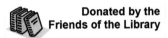

Mrs. God

Mrs. God

PETER STRAUB

PEGASUS CRIME
NEW YORK

MRS. GOD

Pegasus Crime is an Imprint of
Pegasus Books LLC
80 Broad Street, 5th Floor
New York, NY 10004

Copyright © 1990 by Peter Straub

This novel first appeared as part of *Houses Without Doors*

First Pegasus Books cloth edition 2012

Interior design by Maria Fernandez

Library of Congress Cataloging-in-Publication Data is available.

ISBN: 978-1-60598-304-2

10 9 8 7 6 5 4 3 2 1

Printed in the United States of America
Distributed by W. W. Norton & Company

For Lila Kalinich

one

Take a line. What is it about? What is it referring to? What picture can I think of to replace it?

It is as if it doesn't care about me but just stares. (He, She,——.) (Trees, Rocks, Planets, Stars.) Still, I am inside it as much as under or across. I stare back at myself.
—CHARLES BERNSTEIN, Content's Dream

Standish had not realized how tense he was until the jet finally left the ground and his body, as if by itself, began to relax. Nothing could call him back now, neither Jean's anxiety nor his own reservations. It was settled; he was on his way. The startlingly graphic map of lights that was New York City appeared in the window to his left, then slipped out of view. They were at some alarming, dreamlike attitude to the earth that would have meant certain death during Isobel Standish's day—but what might she, in whose name her almost-grandson had ditched both home and seven-months-pregnant wife, not have done with the experience of being revolved above the earth in a metal tube?

The anxiety of the past months continued to ebb from him. Like sweat or semen, anxiety was a physical substance that poured from a self-replenishing well. Of course he was right to go, even Jean had eventually agreed that Esswood was a wonderful opportunity for them both. Three or four weeks at Esswood could lay the groundwork for his tenure, for a book about Isobel—his almost-grandmother—for the whole next stage of his life. When he returned he ought to be carrying in his briefcase the germ of a secured future as surely as Jean once again carried another kind of future life within her womb. And to put it crudely, his would pay for hers.

On the strength of that comfort, he ordered a martini from the stewardess. Of course some of his anxiety had been caused by Esswood itself. Esswood had been known to withdraw its Fellowships, occasionally at times very awkward for the prospective Fellow. The Seneschals, Esswood's owners, appeared to be almost fabulously remote from the details of American academe, but Standish had known two men who, after a period of discreet crowing about being accepted for a term at Esswood, had abruptly ceased to speak about it at all. They had been thrown out before ever getting there.

Ten years ago the first of these, Chester Ridgeley, had been one of the tenured faculty at little Popham College in Popham,

Ohio, where Standish had begun his academic career—a stiffly eccentric, prematurely aged fixture of the English Department, Ridgeley had been invited to spend a sabbatical semester in Esswood's famous library going over notes and drafts of poems by the obscure Georgian poet Theodore Corn, who thirty years before that had been the subject of his dissertation. Theodore Corn had apparently been a frequent guest at Esswood, and once had actually said that no one who had not seen Esswood House and its grounds—"the far field and lazy mill beyond the plangency of pond"—could fully understand his poetry.

"There's nothing quite like it," another faculty member, at the time still thought to be a friend, had said to Standish— the trusting young Standish. "The place is nearly a secret, in spite of everything they're supposed to have in that library. It's still privately owned, and the Seneschals accept only one or two researchers every year. Apparently it's changed a good deal from the glory days when Edith Seneschal ruled the roost and artists made merry in the West Wing, not to mention the hayloft. The family still lives there, but in straitened circumstances—even rather *odd* circumstances, one gathers." He was in every sense a great gatherer, this treacherous so-called friend. Slyly, foxlike, he gathered and gathered. "Ridgeley was lucky—six months to putter around in that great library, discovering crates of unpublished stuff by that ninny Theodore Corn. He'll be able to soak up the landscape around Esswood House, which is supposed to be stunning. And maybe he'll discover the secret. For there is supposed to be a secret, you know. Very clever of our Chester."

Because he had not yet been certain, Standish had not replied to this sly supposed friend, his name and his person both redolent of cough lozenges, that his own grandmother's sister, his grandfather's first wife, had been a guest of the Seneschals at Esswood. He could not even be certain that it was not the allusion to secrecy and a secret that put the notion in his mind. But he thought he remembered that his grandmother's sister had died at an English country house whose name was similar to that of Ridgeley's benefactor; he made no more connection than these two dim coincidences. In those days at Popham, coincidence was still possible.

Just before the end of the fall semester, Standish saw Ridgeley in the English Department office and had to suppress an involuntary gasp of dismay. Ridgeley's scholarly stoop was a positive hunch, his fallen cheeks looked gray, and his eyelids sagged to reveal hectic pink linings. Never truly steady on his feet, now he shuffled like a sick old man. According to Standish's informed hypothetical friend, Ridgeley had sublet his apartment and arranged to store his goods only to be informed that the Seneschal family had learned of certain indiscretions in his history and were regretfully impelled, as they had put it, to withdraw for the immediate future his invitation to join them as an Esswood Fellow.

Indiscretions? Standish asked. Ridgeley?

Well, said his friend, apparently there was some talk about Ridgeley a long time ago. This man, this false pseudofriend whose named evoked the humble lozenge, a corrupt and musky forty-six to Standish's dewy twenty-four, had heard in his first years at Popham only the last echoes of an ambiguous, long-dead situation too vague to be called a scandal. Ridgeley might have mishandled an affair with a student; the student might have chucked her studies and returned to a bleak hometown and died, perhaps even in childbirth. Nothing was certain. For his part, Ridgeley had denied everything and then wisely refused to speak about the situation. The question was, said the treacherous pseudofriend, how had the people at Esswood learned of this musty old affair? Did they hire private detectives? Ridgeley's term at Esswood had not been withdrawn absolutely but only for an unspecified number of terms—maybe they learned no more than Standish. You have to grant, said the foul seducer, that they take themselves very seriously.

Of course Ridgeley had survived, had been able to cancel his sabbatical and keep his apartment and his job; but as far as Standish knew, the summons to Esswood had never been renewed.

The other case came after a fantastic act of betrayal that resulted in bloodshed, real bloodshed, though the blood in question was neither Standish's nor the serpent-friend's, also after the loss of a certain THING, a THING never to be regarded as human but lost indeed, most powerfully and irrevocably lost, wrapped in the bloodied sheets and discarded, burnt or flushed away into psychic oblivion. The other consequence of the act of betrayal had been Standish's eventual removal and appointment to a far, far superior college: Zenith College, in Zenith, Illinois. Standish never understood how Jeremy had managed to get invited to Esswood in the first place—Jeremy Starger, a naive untrustworthy twenty-five-year-old instructor in English, fresh from Ann Arbor with a Ph.D., often literally reeling from drink in the early afternoon. Jeremy's bright little eyes popped and jiggled above his rufous beard as he discoursed inordinately, unstoppably about D. H. Lawrence, the subject of his "research" and the object of his passion. Lawrence had spent several weeks at Esswood, his visits timed so as not to coincide with those of Theodore Corn, whom he detested. (Lawrence had called Corn a "beetle" and a "maggot" in letters to Bertrand Russell.) Standish was surprised that Jeremy knew of Esswood's continuing existence, even more surprised to be buttonholed in a corridor of Zenith's Humanities Building and told that he, Jeremy, had been "taken on" as an Esswood Fellow. Three months, beginning in mid-June. Standish, who was under considerable pressure to complete his own Ph.D., had become acutely aware of Esswood by this time.

After this news Jeremy became increasingly erratic. He often canceled or failed to meet his classes. One day Standish had seen a slim gray envelope in Jeremy's departmental mail slot, its printed return address—at which Standish peeked—only Esswood Foundation, Esswood, Beaswick, Lincolnshire. He had taught a class and returned to the office just as Jeremy, flushed and jubilant, opened the envelope and pulled out the letter. Standish lounged nearer and noticed that it was handwritten. Jeremy glanced at the letter, then sat down heavily in another man's chair. When he saw Standish's inquiring look, he flushed even more darkly and said, "They've reconsidered."

"Oh, no," Standish said. "I'm very sorry, of course."

"Sure, I just bet you are," Jeremy said. "The only emotions you feel, Standish, are—" He stopped talking and shook his head. "I'm sorry. I'm upset. I can't *believe* this. Maybe it's a mistake." He reread the letter. "How could they do this?"

"I gather they can be unpredictable," Standish said. Jeremy's attack made him feel stiff and formal. "Do they give any reason for withdrawing your Fellowship?"

"It has become necessary for us to reconsider your appointment," Jeremy read. *"We apologize for the undoubted inconvenience this must cause you, and offer our sincerest regrets that we shall not be seeing you in England this summer."* Jeremy crumpled the letter into a ball and tossed it into his wastebasket.

"I don't really suppose you know anything about this, do you, Standish?"

"What could I know?" Standish asked. "If someone wrote to the Seneschals that their D. H. Lawrence scholar might spend more time in the local public house than the famous library? I don't know anyone who would do that."

Jeremy bared his teeth at him and stormed out, undoubtedly on his way to the Stein, the bar most favored by Zenith's faculty.

A year later the effusive Jeremy had exiled himself to an Assistant Professorship in central Oklahoma, and William Standish had begun to realize what Esswood could do for him. His investigations into the poetry written by his grandfather Martin's first wife had led him to believe that this restless, impatient woman, completely unknown, had been an important precursor of Modernism—a lost talent, minor but significant. If she had spent weekends at Garsington, if she had *died* at Garsington, where half of Bloomsbury plus T. S. Eliot would have celebrated her, taken her under its angelic, malicious wings, above all promoted her, she would now be a famous poet. But Isobel Standish had spent weekends with Edith Seneschal instead of Ottoline Morrell, and had died and remained obscure. (Theodore Corn spent entire months at Garsington, but compared to Isobel, Corn was a mellifluous blockhead.)

Isobel Standish had published only one book, the slender *Crack, Whack, and Wheel*, Brunton Press, 1912. Half of its five hundred copies had been donated to libraries or distributed to friends. The remainder, unnoticed, unreviewed, was left cased in the basement on Brunton Street in Duxbury, Massachusetts, of Martin Standish, who had paid for the publication of his wife's odd little book. It must have looked very odd indeed to unliterary Martin. To William Standish's more educated eye, the poems were astonishingly original, using speech rhythms, nonsense passages, irregular lines, gnomic diction. This poetry implicitly rebuked sentimentality and celebrated its own off-center gravity. Isobel Standish deserved to take her place among Stevens, Moore, Williams, Pound, and Eliot. She was in some ways the Emily Dickinson of the twentieth century; and she was William Standish's private property.

By this time he had come to realize that his dissertation on Henry James had quietly expired. He was still married, and though he and Jean were again now able, after all their trials, to think about trying to become parents, his career at Zenith was growing more imperiled year by year. Two books about Isobel Standish, an edition of her complete work edited by himself and a consideration of her place in contemporary poetry, would satisfy the tenure committee and enable him to keep his job. He could make an end run around the ghastly corpse of his dissertation and then fly free of Zenith altogether—to come to rest in some far more suitable, even ivied, world.

Nine months before the committee had informed him that publication of some kind would be an absolute requirement of his staying on at Zenith, he had written to Esswood inquiring if in fact Isobel had enjoyed the hospitality of the Seneschals, if she had worked at Esswood—above all, if she had left papers in the celebrated library. If so, might this letter be considered an application for a Fellowship of whatever duration Esswood might deem most appropriate for a thorough study of her work? He had not neglected to describe his enthusiasm for Isobel's work and his sense of its importance, nor to allude to his odd relationship to the poet.

Esswood had returned a prompt acknowledgment signed with the initials R. W. His application would be decided upon "in due course." Standish informed the members of the committee that he expected to have news for them soon and allowed them to conclude from that what they might.

Three months went by without word from England. In January, the fifth month, Jean Standish learned that she was pregnant again and that the child was due in late September. In the third month of her pregnancy Jean developed alarming symptoms—high blood pressure, one unaccountable instance of vaginal bleeding—and was ordered into bed for four weeks. She dutifully took to her bed. At the end of this time, eight weeks after his application, Standish finally received another letter from Beaswick, Lincolnshire. He had been accepted. For a period of three weeks, he was to be given free access to the Isobel Standish papers and whatever else he might find helpful. ("We do not believe in unnecessary circumscriptions on scholarly work," wrote R. W., now revealed as one Robert Wall.) Robert Wall had added a bland sentence of apology for the delay, which went unexplained. Standish thought that they had offered the Fellowship during August to someone else, and the other person had eventually turned them down. Or they had withdrawn their appointment, as with Jeremy Starger and Chester Ridgeley. This seemed more likely. Someone else's failure had been his salvation.

For salvation it was. Standish's chairman agreed to postpone for a year any decision about his future at Zenith College. Within that time Standish was to prepare his edition of Isobel's work, write a lengthy introduction, and arrange for publication of the volume.

Jean had been the last obstacle. How do you know they won't withdraw it at the last minute? Maybe they do this all the time. (Unfortunately, Jean knew all about Chester Ridgeley and Jeremy Starger.) Have you ever known anyone who actually went there? Maybe the whole place is a fantastic practical joke, maybe it's just another one of your crazy fantasies, maybe they'll find out about *you*. Don't you think about that, Bill? Why do you need them, anyhow? Flushed, fearful, Jean woke him at night and drilled questions at him until she, not he, broke down into tears of doubt. The next day she adopted an uncharacteristic meekness, barely speaking when he returned to the apartment after school—she was a walking apology.

When he said that he was taking the appointment for the sake of their shared future, she said, "Don't pretend that you want to go for my sake." During the final months of the semester, Jean wavered between a meek deceptive acceptance of his plans and an increasingly violent opposition to them. By June, she wept whenever either of them mentioned the trip. It was impossible for him to leave—especially now. There were other colleges besides Zenith. And even if no other colleges would hire him, weren't there always high schools? Would that be such a disgrace?

And what if I lose this baby? Don't you realize it could happen?

But she never said, And what if I lose this baby too? And she never blamed him, except perhaps once, for the loss of the THING wrapped in the bloody sheets and flushed away into null-world, oblivion.

Sometimes during these weeks Standish looked at his obese wife, her hair hanging in loose damp disarray around her red face and wondered who she was, who it was that he had married. He reminded her that she was healthy, that he would be back three weeks before the birth.

You won't, she said. *I know it. I'll be all alone in the hospital, and I'll die.*

If it's that bad, he finally told her, I'll write to Esswood and tell them I can't go because of problems at home.

You think I'm bullying you, you're so weak, you don't understand, you don't even remember.

What don't I understand?

This baby is real. Real! I am going to have this baby! Do you know for certain there is an Esswood? How can you be so sure you'll write a book there?

Especially, she meant, since you've never been able to write one here at home.

Do you remember, do you, do you, do you, do you even remember what you made me do?

It doesn't matter, Standish thought, in a week or two I'll get the flat gray envelope with its single handwritten paragraph.

He sat with Jean in the evenings. He talked about his classes, they watched television. Jean spoke of very little but food, soap operas, and the movements of the baby in her womb. She seemed two-dimensional, like someone who had died and been imperfectly resurrected. One night he took his *Crack, Whack, and Wheel* from the shelf and began making notes. Jean did not protest. Oddly, the poems seemed lifeless to him, untalented and childish. They too seemed dead.

The gray envelope would come any day, he thought, and put an end to this charade. Mail came to the department office between three and three-thirty, and each day after his Freshman class Standish approached the office with a familiar heartsickness. He looked at the slot bearing his name as soon as he came through the door.

After six working days he found a gray envelope in the slot. It bore the return address of the Esswood Foundation. Standish glanced reflexively toward the littered desk that had been Jeremy Starger's, and the bearded young eighteenth-century specialist who used it now looked up at him and frowned. "Keep away from me, Standish," he said. Not bothering to reply, Standish took the envelope from his slot, along with the bundle of publishers' announcements that was his usual mail. He was surprised to find how disappointed, almost frightened, he was. Standish dropped the textbook announcements into the overflowing departmental wastebasket and carried the gray envelope to his desk. He felt hot. He knew he was blushing. Robert Wall had found him out. Sighing, he ripped open the envelope and pulled out a sheet of hieroglyphic nonsense which after a few seconds resolved itself into a mimeographed map illustrating how to drive from Heathrow Airport to Beaswick, where Esswood was located. His heartbeat and his flush faded. A lightly penciled *X* marked Esswood's location. Standish felt the profound relief of one who after being sentenced to death receives a full pardon.

That night he gave the map to Jean as she sat before the television set. "Nice," she said, and held it out toward him. In the glare from the set her cheeks were as puffy as bolsters. As Jean's belly had expanded, so had the rest of her body, encasing her in an unhappy overcoat made of ice cream and doughnuts. He took the map from her bloated fingers. He imagined that Isobel Standish had remained slim all her life.

". . . good it's going to do," she muttered to the screen.

"What?"

"I wonder how much good that map is going to do you." She did not bother to look at him.

"Why would you wonder about that?" he asked, unable to keep a sudden quickening from his voice.

"Because it shows you how to get to that place from Heathrow." Then she did turn her head to face him.

"Heathrow is the name of the London airport."

"But you're not going to London. You're going to someplace called Gatwick."

The name Gatwick did sound familiar. Standish went upstairs to the bedroom, pulled his airline ticket out of his dresser drawer, and read what was printed on its face.

"You're right," he said when he came back downstairs. Jean grunted. Standish wondered if she had prowled through his dresser drawers. The television seemed very loud. He turned to the bookshelf and pulled out an atlas and found the index for England. Gatwick was unlisted.

Standish sat down in the chair beside Jean's and unfolded Robert Wall's little map, with its complications of roadways and interchanges. None of the towns in black boldface was Gatwick. He could see Gatwick nowhere between London and Lincolnshire. Gatwick was literally off the map. Well, he would find the place once he got there. Gas stations all had maps. England had to have gas stations, didn't it?

Though Standish checked his mail every day, Robert Wall never wrote that Esswood had found it necessary to withdraw his appointment; and now here he was, thirty thousand feet above the Atlantic Ocean. Standish had two more drinks on the long flight, and nearly ordered a fourth until he remembered Jeremy Starger.

You couldn't turn a ridiculous red-bearded little drunk loose in the Esswood library, could you? You couldn't let that happen.

Standish took *Crack, Whack, and Wheel* from his carry-on bag. Feeling pleasantly honorable and muzzy from gin, he opened Isobel's book. His underlinings, notes, and annotations jumped reassuringly out at him, testimony to the merits of Isobel's poetry and the depth of his own thought. Here were the physical traces of an alert scholarly mind at work on a worthy object. *Cf. Psalm 69,* read one of his notes, *world does not answer the cry for pity, ironic intent, ref. husband?* In ink of another color, he had added *eloquent offer of charity, attribute of the poetic self.* And in pencil above this was added *antinarrative strategy.* Isobel Standish's work was full of antinarrative strategy. At some point Standish had scrawled *Odysseus, Dante* in the crowded margins. The title of the poem he had annotated so industriously was "Rebuke."

Neither found he any, the vagrant said
Under the moldering eaves of the house
Full of heaviness and no one to comfort,
No one wavering up to say

"Put on your indiscretions, little fool,
but first take your glasses off. Why, Miss Standish . . ."
This glowing moon. The crowd
Has already gathered on the terraces.

The history of one who came too late
To the rooms of broken babies and their toys
Is all they talk about around here
And rebuke, did you think you'd be left out?

Blurry with a hangover, he ate the terrible airline meal, drank one glass of red wine that tasted of solvent, and nursed another through the movie. He was not accustomed to drinking so much. Jean did not approve of wine with meals, and Standish did not usually appreciate the sluggishness and confusion with which more than a single drink afflicted him. Yet this was not at all the life to which he was accustomed—the safety of home was thousands of miles behind him, and he was suspended in midair with a copy of *Crack, Whack, and Wheel,* on his way somewhere utterly unknown. Every aspect of this circumstance felt ripe with anxiety. Three weeks seemed a very long time to be immured in a remote country house looking at manuscripts of poems he still was not sure he understood.

Standish fell asleep during the movie, and woke up in dim morning greasy with sweat, as if covered with a fine film of oil.

The stewardess had put a blanket over him, and he thrashed and kicked, imagining that some loathsome thing, some fragment of a nightmare, lay atop him—fully awake, he wiped his greasy face with his hands and looked around. Only a few goggling idiots had observed his moment of panic. Standish pulled the blanket off the floor and only then noticed that he had an erection. Like some huge beast diving into concealment, his dream shifted massively just beneath the surface of his memory.

The airplane began to descend shortly after he had eaten. Standish pushed up his window cover, and cold gray light streamed into the cabin. They seemed to descend through layer after layer of this silvery undersea light. At last the plane came through a final layer of clouds filled with a pure, unliving whiteness, and an utterly foreign landscape opened beneath them. Tiny fields as distinct as cobblestones surrounded an equally tiny airport. In the distance, two great motorways met and mingled on the outskirts of a little city surrounded by rows of terraced houses. A long way past the toy city lay a forest, a great flash of vibrant green that seemed the only true color in the landscape. *England,* Standish thought. A thrill of strangeness passed through him.

The plane landed at some distance from the terminal, and the passengers had to carry their hand baggage across the tarmac. Standish's arms ached from the weight of the various small bags he had filled at the last minute with books and cassettes. His Walkman bumped his chest as it swung on its strap. He felt a queer, fatalistic exhilaration. The silvery light, a light never seen in America, lay over the tarmac. Two dwarfish men in filthy boilersuits stood in the shadows beneath the airplane watching the passengers trudge toward the terminal. Standish knew that if he could overhear the words the men passed as they squinted through their cigarette smoke, he would not understand a one.

But he had no trouble understanding or being understood as he passed through the airport. The customs official treated him courteously, and the Immigration Officer seemed genuinely interested in Standish's response to the question about the purpose of his visit. And when Standish asked him for directions to a village in Lincolnshire, he said, "Don't worry, sir. This is a small country, compared to yours. You can't get too lost." Every word, in fact every syllable of this charming little speech was not only clear but musical: the Immigration Officer's voice rose and fell as did no American's, and so did that of the girl behind the rental desk, who had never heard of Esswood or Beaswick but pressed several maps on him before she walked him to the terminal's glass doors and pointed to the decade-old turquoise Ford Escort, humble and patient as a mule, he had rented. "The boot should hold all your bags," she said, "but there's lashings of room in the backseat, if not. You'll want to begin on the motorway directly ahead and go straight through the interchange, that'll see you on your way."

Standish wondered if all over England people played tunes at you with their voices.

two

Driving on the left, so counter to his instincts, elated him. Like all driving it was largely a matter of fitting in with the stream. Standish found that it took only a small adjustment to switch on the radio with the left hand instead of the right, to pass slower cars on the wrong side—but he was not sure how long this control would last in an emergency. If the car ahead of him blew a tire or began to skid . . . Standish saw himself creating a monumental crack-up, a line of wrecked smoking cars extending back a mile. His heart was beating fast, and he smiled at himself in the rearview mirror. He was tired and jet-lagged, but he felt foolishly, shamelessly alive.

Only the roundabouts gave him trouble. The stream of traffic swept him into a great whirling circle from which drivers were to choose alternate exits marked by a great spoke-like diagram. At first Standish could not tell which of the spokes was his, and drove sweating around the great circle twice. When at last he had seen that he wanted the third of the exits, he found himself trapped in the roundabout's inner lane, unable to break through the circling traffic. He went around once more, straining to look over his shoulder, and set the windshield wipers slapping back and forth before he located the turn indicator. As soon as he began to move out of his lane several horns blared at once. Standish swore and twisted the wheel back. Around once more he went, and this time managed to enter the stream of cars on the outer edge of the roundabout. When he squirted into the exit his entire body was damp with sweat.

Twenty-five miles further north, the whole thing happened all over again. His map slipped on the seat, and he panicked—he was supposed to stay on this northbound motorway, but at some point he did have to turn off onto a trunk road, and from that onto a series of roads that were only thin black lines on the map. He drove around and around and doubt overwhelmed him. His turn indicator ticked like a bomb. Sweat loosened his grip on the wheel. At last he managed to penetrate the honking wall of cars and escape the roundabout. He pulled off to the side of the road and scrabbled amongst the maps strewn on the floor. When he had the proper map in his hands, he could not locate the roundabout he had just fled. It did not exist on the map, only in life. His earlier feelings of relaxation and purposefulness mocked him now. They were illusions; he was lost. At length the desire to weep left him and he calmed down. He found a roundabout on the map, an innocuous gray circle, which almost had to be the one he had just escaped. He was not supposed to get off the motorway for another sixty miles, where a sign should indicate the way to Huckstall, the village where he picked up the next road. He would not have to brave any more roundabouts. Standish pulled out into the traffic.

After a time, the landscape became astonishingly empty. Dung-colored bushes lay scattered across flat colorless land. Far away in the distance was a gathering of red brick cottages. Standish wondered if this might be Huckstall.

He looked at the tiny village through the passenger window and saw a pale face pressed against a second-floor window, a white blur surrounded by black just as if—really for all the world, Standish thought, just as if a child had been imprisoned in that ugly two-story building, walled up within the red brick to stare eternally toward the cars rushing past on the motorway. Smaller white blotches that might have been hands pressed against the glass, and a hole opened up in the bottom of the child's face, as if the child were screaming at Standish, screaming for help!

He quickly looked away and saw that a low black hill had appeared before him on the right side of the motorway. Bare of vegetation, the hill seemed to fasten onto the empty landscape rather than grow from it. Other hills like it canceled half the horizon. They looked dead, like garbage piles—then he thought they looked like black blood-soaked sheets, bloody towels and pads thrown onto the abortionist's floor.

The air carried a sour metallic tang, as if it were filled with
tiny metal shavings. Standish came up beside the first low hill
and saw that it was a mound of some material like charcoal
briquets—stony chips of coal. Now and then rock slides of
the chips ran down the flanks of the hill. Between the black
hills of coal dusty men rode toylike bulldozers. Completely
ringed by the black hills was a world of men rushing around
in blackened, murky air beneath strings of lights. Obscure
machines rose and fell. Yellow flares burned beside the black
mounds. *Slag heaps,* Standish thought, not knowing if he was
right. What were slag heaps, anyhow?

Even the sky seemed dirty. Rhythmic clanks and thuds as
from underground machines filled the air. It was like driving
through a hellish factory without walls or roof. Standish had
not seen a road sign or marker for what must have been miles.
There was nothing around him now but the shifting black hills
and the dusty men moving between the flares. Suddenly the
road seemed too narrow to be the motorway.

He decided to keep driving until he saw a road sign. The
thought of getting out of his car in this brutal and desolate
place made his throat tighten.

Then the entire world changed in an eye-blink. The black
hills, strings of lights, men on toy bulldozers, and tiny flares
fell back behind him, and Standish found himself driving
through dense, vibrant green. On either side of the car fat
vine-encrusted trees and wide bushes pushed right to the
edge of the road. For ten or fifteen minutes Standish drove
through what appeared to be a great forest. The interior
of the car grew as hot as a greenhouse. Standish pulled up
to the side of the road and wiped his forehead. Leaves and

vines flattened against the side window. He looked at his map again.

Northeast from the second roundabout extended the road to Huckstall. The map indicated woodlands in green, but none of the green covered the roadway. Sickeningly, Standish thought that all this right-left business had so confused him that he had traveled south from Gatwick instead of north— by now he would be hundreds of miles out of his way. He groaned and closed his eyes. Something soft thumped against his windshield. Standish moaned in dismay and surprise, and reflexively covered his face with his arms.

He lowered his arms and looked out. On the upper right-hand side of the windshield was a broad smeary stripe which he did not think had been there earlier. Standish did not at all want to think about what sort of creature had made the smear. An insect the size of a baby had turned to froth and spread itself like butter across the glass. Death again, messy and uncontainable. He wiped his face and started forward again.

The woodland ended as abruptly as it had begun, and without any transition Standish found himself back in the empty burnt-looking landscape. Twice he passed through other, smaller outdoor factories with their slag heaps and dusty men wandering through flares. He felt as if he had been driving in circles. There were no signs to Huckstall or anywhere else. Unmarked roads intersected his, leading deeper into the undulating russet landscape. *Full of heaviness and no one to comfort,* Standish remembered from "Rebuke." He longed for markers pointing to Boston or Sleaford or Lincoln, names prominent on the map Robert Wall had sent him.

In minutes a low marker, a small stone post like a tooth set upright beside the road, came into view before him. Standish pulled up across from it. He got out of the car and walked around to see the worn words carved on the marker: 12MI. Twelve miles? Twelve miles from what?

"Lost?"

Standish snapped his head up to see a tall thin man standing directly behind the little stone tooth. He might just now have jumped up out of the earth. His loose baggy brown trousers, spattered boots, and rumpled mackintosh were nearly the color of the landscape. He wore a dark cap pulled low on his forehead. The man slouched and grinned at Standish. He was missing most of his teeth.

"I don't really know," Standish said.

"Is that right?" said the grinning man. His tongue licked the spaces between his teeth.

"I mean, I'm trying to figure it out," Standish said. "I thought this marker might help me."

"And does it?" The man's voice was a sly quiet burr, remarkably insinuating. "There's precise matter to be read here. A man might do a great deal with information as accurate as that."

Standish hated the man's dry, insulting mockery. "Well, it doesn't do me any good. I thought I was on the motorway, going toward Huckstall."

"Huckstall." The man pondered it. "Never heard of Americans making their way to Huckstall."

"I'm not really going *to* Huckstall," Standish said, infuriated at having to explain himself. "I just thought I might have lunch there. I was going to pick up the road to Lincolnshire."

"Lincolnshire, is it? You'll want to do a good bit of driving. And you thought you were on the motorway. Is this how motorways look in America, then?"

"Where *is* the motorway?" Standish cried.

"Kill a bird? Little baby?"

"What?"

"With your car?" He pointed his chin toward the smear on the windshield.

"You're crazy," Standish said, though he had feared exactly this.

The man blinked and stepped backward. His tongue slid into one of the spaces between his teeth. Now he seemed uncertain and defensive instead of insolent. He was crazy, after all—Standish had been too startled to see it.

"Where are you from?" he asked, hoping that the man would answer: Huckstall.

The man tilted his head back over his shoulder, indicating wide empty blankness. Then he took another backward step, as if he feared that Standish might try to capture him. The stranger came into focus for Standish: he was not at all the ironic, almost menacing figure he had seemed. The fellow was deficient, probably retarded. He lived in that empty wilderness and he slept in his clothes. Now that he was no longer afraid of the man, Standish could pity him.

"Killed something, that'll do you," the man said. His eyes gleamed like a dog's, and he edged a bit further away. "That'll be bad luck, that will."

Standish thought the bad luck was in meeting an oaf straight out of Thomas Hardy. "Where is Huckstall, would you know?"

"I would. That I would. Yes."

"And?"

"And?"

"And where is it?" Standish shouted.

"Up there, up there, right up that road, which is the very road you're on."

Standish sighed.

"They flee from me," the man said.

Standish put his hands in his pockets and began to move around the front of the car without quite turning his back on the vagrant.

"That sometime did me seek," the man said. "With naked foot, stalking in my chamber."

Standish stopped moving, aware that he was, after all, in England. No addled American tramp would quote Thomas Wyatt at you. The English teacher in him was piqued and delighted. "Go on," he said.

"I have seen them gentle, tame, and meek, That now are wild and do not once remember, That sometime . . ." He paused, then intoned, *"Timor mortis conturbat me,"* quoting from another poem. Evidently he was a ragbag of disconnected phrases.

"Hah! Very good," Standish said, smiling. "Excellent. You've been very helpful to me. Thank you."

The man closed his eyes and began to chant. "In going to my naked bed as one that would have *slept,* I heard a wife saying to her child, that long before had *wept,* She sighed sad and sang full sweet, to bring the babe to *rest,* That would not calm but cried still, in sucking at her *breast."*

"Um, yes," Standish said, and quickly got into the car. He turned the key in the ignition and glanced sideways at the man, who had come out of his trance and was shuffling toward the car, reaching for the handle of the passenger door. Standish cursed himself for not locking the doors as soon as he had gotten in. The engine caught, and Standish pulled away before the man reached the handle. He looked in the mirror and saw the creature staggering up the middle of the road, gesturing with both hands. Standish looked ahead quickly.

He drove through the emptiness for perhaps five minutes before coming to a small green sign which read HUCKSTALL 10MI.

It was, when he came to it, a village of narrow lanes lined with brick cottages, so ugly and uninviting that he nearly decided to pass through it and continue on. But the next village appeared to be at least twenty miles away, and it would take forty-five minutes to drive that distance over the country roads. And when he came up to the market square in the center of town, Huckstall did not seem so grim.

Triangular plastic pennants on strings marked off separate areas of the cobbled square—on market days, each area would belong to a separate stallholder. Beyond the strings of pennants lay reassuring signs of civilization, a bow-fronted shop called Boots the Chemist, the imperial stone facade of a Lloyds Bank, and the plate-glass window, filled with brightly colored paperbacks, of a W. H. Smith bookstore. On the corner opposite Standish and his Escort crammed with luggage stood a large double-fronted half-timbered building with bay windows, a small blue sign with the words TAKE COURAGE below a golden rooster, and a much larger sign depicting crossed dueling pistols which bore the legend THE DUELISTS. The windows sparkled, the blue paint and white trim gleamed. Standish had a sudden vision of a roasted pig on a serving platter, thick wedges of crumbly yellow cheese, overflowing tankards of ale, a fat smiling man in a toque carving slices of rare roast beef and pouring thick brown gravy onto Yorkshire pudding.

He could make it to Beaswick and Esswood in another three or four hours. *Stopped off for a pub lunch,* he would say. *Beautiful little place in Huckstall called The Duelists. Do you know it? Ought to be in the guidebooks, if you ask me.*

Standish left his car parked on the side of the square and walked through the chill gray air toward the glistening pub. His stomach rumbled. It came to him that he had driven a strange car hundreds of unfamiliar miles, he was the recipient of a distinguished English literary fellowship, he was about to enter an English interior for the first time. He fairly bounded up the steps and opened the door.

His first impression was of the pub's size, his second that it must have closed for the afternoon. The interior of The Duelists was divided into a series of enormous rooms furnished with round tables and padded booths. A red plaid carpet covered the floors, and the walls were artificially half-timbered. In the hazy light from the windows, Standish saw a stocky black-haired man washing glasses behind the bar on the far side of the rows of empty tables. The air stank of cigarette smoke. The bartender glanced up at Standish hovering inside the door, then resumed pulling large, vaguely pineapple-shaped glasses out of hot water and setting them up on the bar.

Standish wondered if he still had time to get a sandwich. He walked to the bar. The tops of the tables were slick with beer, and most of the ashtrays were filled. Crumpled packs of Silk Cut and Rothmans lay beside the ashtrays.

"Yes," the barman said, looking up sharply before plunging his hands into the water again.

"Are you open?"

"Door's not locked, is it?"

"No, I thought maybe the licensing laws—"

"Been a change then, has there? And about bloody time, too."

"Well, I wondered—"

The man fixed Standish with an impatient stare, wiped his hands on a towel, and leaned against the bar.

"You're not closed," Standish said.

The man held out both hands palm-up and moved them outward in a gesture that said: See for yourself. "So if you'll place your order, sir . . ."

"Well, I was hoping to get a beer and something to eat, I guess."

"Menu's behind the bar." He tilted his head toward a chalkboard advertising steak and kidney pie, shepherd's pie, ploughman's lunch, ham sandwich, cheese sandwich, Scotch egg, pork pie, batter-fried prawns, and batter-fried scallops.

Standish was charmed all over again. In this list he saw how far he had come from Zenith. He suspected the food might be humble by English standards, but he wanted to taste it all. Here was the simple nutritious food of the people, shepherds and ploughmen.

"It all looks so *good*," he said.

"Oh, aye?" The barman frowned and turned around to look at the chalkboard himself. "You'd better order some of it then, hadn't you?"

"Ploughman's lunch, please." Standish envisioned a big steaming bowl with potatoes and leeks and sausages all mixed up in a rich broth. "It's good, is it?"

"Good enough for some," the barman said. "Chutney or pickle?"

"Why, a little of both."

The man turned and disappeared through a door at the far end of the bar. After a moment Standish realized that he had gone into the kitchen to place the order. The bartender returned as abruptly as he had left—his face had an odd flinty concentrated look that made him seem always to be performing some unwelcome task. "And, sir?"

"And?"

"And what did you want from the bar? Pint of bitter? Half pint?"

"What a wonderful idea!" Standish exclaimed, knowing that he sounded like an idiot but unable to restrain himself. *A pint of bitter.* Standish was suddenly aware of the smallness of England, of its *coziness,* the snugness and security and warmth of this island nation.

The bartender was still staring at him with that tense flinty expression.

"Oh, a pint, I guess," Standish said.

"A pint of what, sir?" He swept his hand toward old-fashioned pump taps with ceramic handles. "The ordin'ry?"

"No, what's the best one? I just got off the plane from the States a couple of hours ago."

The man nodded, picked up one of the pint mugs he had set out to dry, set it beneath a tap marked Director's Bitter, and hauled back on the tap. Cloudy brown liquid spurted out into the glass. The man pushed and pulled the pump until the glass had filled. His face still seemed stretched taut, immobilized, as if a layer of cells deep within had died.

"You folks still drink warm beer over here, is that right?"

"We don't boil it," the bartender said. He thumped the pint on the bar before Standish. "You'll let that settle, sir."

What was still swirling around in the glass looked like something drawn up from a swamp. Little brown silty fecal things spun around and around.

"We don't see many Yanks up this way," he said.

"Oh, I've still got a long way to go," Standish said, watching his beer spin. "I'm on my way to a village called Beaswick. Lincolnshire. I'm invited to a, I guess you'd say, manor house called Esswood."

"The fellow was murdered there," the barman said. "That'll be three pounds forty altogether."

Standish counted out four pounds from his stash of English money. "You must be mistaken," he said. "It's a kind of foundation. Every year they invite someone—you'd have to say it's a kind of honor."

"Funny kind of honor." The barman gave Standish his change. "American, he was. Like yourself, sir." He turned away. "Take a seat, sir. The food will be out directly."

Standish carried the heavy glass to a table in the second rank and sat down. He examined the beer. It was calmer now. A thin layer of foam lay on its top like scum. The spinning brown things had dissolved into the murk. He sipped cautiously. Over a strong clear bite of alcohol rode a sharp deep tang more that of whiskey than of beer. It was like drinking some primitive tribal medicine. Standish felt a healthy, cheering distance between himself and the standards of Zenith. He took a longer swallow and told himself he was getting to like this stuff.

"That's strong, that is, the Director's," said a female voice behind him, and Standish jerked his hand in surprise and soaked his cuff with beer.

"Beggin' your pardon," the girl said, smiling at Standish's sudden consternation. She was a pretty blonde in her late teens or early twenties with wide, rather blank eyes of an almost transparent pale blue. She wore a red woolen sweater covered by a stained, bulging white apron that for some reason reminded Standish of a nurse's uniform. He noticed that she was very pregnant before he saw that she was carrying a plate with a large wedge of cheese and the heel of a loaf of French bread. "Your food."

"I'm sorry, but that isn't what I ordered," Standish said.

"Of course you ordered it," she said, all her amusement gone in an instant. "You're the only bloody customer in the place, d'you think I could make a mistake like that with but the one order?"

"Wait. This is cheese and—"

"Ploughman's lunch, that is. With pickles *and* chutney." She thrust it before him so that he could see the two puddles of sauce, brown and yellow, beside the wedge of cheese.

She set the plate roughly on the table and rapped a knife and a fork down beside it. "Wouldn't you call that right?" A glance at him. "He came into the kitchen and said, 'Ploughman's lunch, pickle and chutney,' and I said, 'Wants both, does he?' because I'd looked out the window and seen you making for the pub and I knew you were a Yank by your clothes and the way you walked, just like a Yank it was, you needn't think I'm ignorant just because I live in Huckstall and work in a pub, I'm educated better far than your great ignorant American girls, I've two A levels and two O levels, and my husband *owns* this pub, you should see the envy on their faces when we go home, you should see—"

About midway through this astonishing speech Standish became aware of the meaning of the rigid expression on the barman's face: *Not this, not again.* The girl was breathing hard, and she placed one hand on her chest.

"Enough," the barman said from behind Standish.

The girl glared down at Standish and turned away to move quickly through the empty tables, tugging at the tie of the apron as she went. She dropped the apron at the door and pushed through to the outside.

Standish looked up in amazement at the barman. He was wiping his hands on a white towel, and he looked back down at Standish with a stony rigidity.

"Closing time, sir," he said.

"What?"

"You'll be leaving now. Time."

"But I haven't even—"

"Your money will be refunded, sir." He took a crumpled wad of bills from his pocket, found four single pound notes, and set them down on Standish's table, where they immediately wilted in a puddle of spilled beer.

"Oh, come on," Standish said. "I could wait here if you want to go out and bring her back. Honest, I understand—my wife's pregnant too, she said a lot of crazy things just before I left—"

"Time," the man said, and put a hand as heavy as a bag of cement on Standish's shoulder. "Take the cheese. I am closing now, sir."

Standish gulped down a mouthful of the awful beer. He stood. The barman slid his hand down Standish's arm to his elbow. "Now, sir, please."

"You don't have to push me out!" Standish grabbed the wedge of cheese as the barman began to move him toward the door. The man's face was concentrated and expressionless, as if he were moving a heavy piece of furniture.

He permitted Standish to open the door of the pub.

Outside in the bright gray air, Standish looked down at the empty market square with its fluttering flags. The pregnant girl had disappeared. Standish heard the clanking of heavy bolts behind him.

"Jesus," he said. He looked down at the pie-shaped wedge of cheese. From somewhere came a pervasive distant thunder like the noise of a hidden turbine. It seemed to him that people were peering at him from behind curtains.

He looked across the square. A shiny, half-flattened bag flipped across the cobbles in a moist breeze, dribbling out crumbled potato chips and white chunks of salt. The cheese in his hand had begun to adhere to his fingers.

Of course, he thought. In a place this size everybody knows everything—that crazy woman chased them all out of the pub before I showed up. They were waiting to see how long I'd last.

The homely little turquoise mule across the square sat in a dazzle and sparkle of water or of quartz embedded into the cobbles. Standish walked toward it along the perimeter of the square. Other people's lives were like novels, he thought. You saw so little, you had only a peek through a window and then you had to guess about what you had seen.

For a moment, he quite clearly saw before him the pretty quadrangle, crisscrossed by intersecting paths, that was the center of the Popham campus.

At a scuffle of movement behind him he turned around and nearly stumbled. The crowd he had imagined was not there. In an arch between The Duelists and a tobacconist's shop he glimpsed two people watching—a blonde woman in a red jersey and a tall man in a cap and a long muddy coat. It took Standish a moment to realize why this man looked familiar: he was the tramp who had startled him on the road to Huckstall. They vanished beneath an arch. Standish heard the footsteps of the tramp and the publican's wife clattering down the hidden street.

But the tramp had been twelve miles out of town. He could not have walked so far in the short time since Standish had seen him.

They flee from me that sometime did me seek.

He jumped at a sudden noise, and saw only the shiny bag flipping over the stones. The odd rumbling of unseen engines persisted.

Standish looked at the darkened pub and saw the source of the mysterious sound. Beyond the top of the pub, the distance of a field away, a steady stream of trucks and cars rolled north on an elevated road. It was the motorway he had managed to lose at one of the roundabouts.

The rest of the drive to Lincolnshire passed with what seemed to him surprising ease. The motorways swept him uneventfully toward his destination; the tangle of lines on Robert Wall's map resolved itself, after frequent inspection, into actual roads with actual identities that led to actual places; he lost his way only once, by overshooting a badly marked intersection. By all his earlier standards, it was a difficult and confusing journey, but by the standards of the morning, it was nearly painless.

The light faded. In the growing darkness Standish began to see dikes and canals in the fields, which even in the diminishing light were of a glowing, almost electrical green. The map led him past tiny Lincolnshire villages and through broad marshes. A pale phosphorescence, as of something dead come back to uneasy life, now and then glowed far off in the marshes.

He came to Beaswick in the dark, at ten o'clock at night. The village was a mean affair of ugly row houses interspersed with pubs and chip shops. In ten minutes he had passed through it, still following his map.

A few minutes later he came to an unmarked road that led into a darkness of massive oaks. He drove through an iron gate opened onto a drive that went looping through the monumental trees. He rounded a final curve and saw before him an immense white house at the top of a wide flight of steps. Behind the house his headlights shone upon a descending series of terraces before they flashed across the windows of the house. Standish pulled up before the steps and got out of his car. When he took his first long look at Esswood House, an entirely unforeseen thing happened to him. He fell in love with it.

three

S tandish had never been to France or Italy, he had never seen Longliet, Hardwick Hall, Wilton House, or any of the twenty country estates that were Esswood's equal; it would have made no difference if he had. Esswood struck him as perfect. The clear symmetrical line of the house, broken regularly by great windows, delighted him. He tried to remember the name for a facade like this, but the word would not come. It did not matter. The whole great white structure seemed balanced, in harmony with itself and the countryside around it. What might have been forbidding—the whiteness and severity of its facade, the flight of steps that might have reminded him of a government building—had been humanized by constant use.

A single family, the Seneschals, had lived here for hundreds of years. People had moved familiarly up and down these steps and through every one of the rooms. Generations of children had grown up here. Even in the darkness the stairs showed worn patches, eroded by generations of Seneschals and hundreds of poets and painters and novelists. Here and there the paint was flaking, and water damage had left dark linear stains at the corners of some of the noble windows. These small blemishes did not disturb Esswood's perfection.

Standish opened the trunk of the car and lifted out two of his large suitcases. They seemed much heavier than they had in Zenith, and Standish dropped them one after the other onto the gravel before he closed his trunk. Then he picked them up and trudged toward the staircase.

Someone in the house heard the sounds he made as he struggled toward the door. A light passed down the row of dark windows at the front of the house and moved toward the door. Standish wondered if a servant girl were rushing toward Esswood's main entrance with a lighted candle, as would have happened centuries earlier. Would they still have servant girls, he wondered, and then began to wonder if he should be using the main entrance. There had to be an entrance at ground level, probably beside the staircase or off to the side of the house, where he had seen a trellised arbor. He grunted and hauled the two big suitcases up onto the terrace atop the steps. The massive, heavily ornamented door opened onto a blaze of light and color, and a woman in a well-cut gray pin-striped suit with a tight-fitting skirt stepped back, smiling to welcome him in. She appeared to be about his own age or slightly older, with long loosely bound hair and an intelligent hawklike face with bright animated eyes.

Anxiety and surprise undid him. He said, "Is this the right door? Did I come to the right place?"

"Mr. Standish," the woman said. Her voice was warm and soothing. "We've been wondering where you might be. Please come in."

He fell another notch deeper into infatuation with Esswood.

"I've been wondering where I might be, too," he said, and thought he saw a flash of approval in her lively eyes. Then he ruined it. "This where they all come in? This is the right door?" She nodded, smiling now at his fatuity instead of his wit, and he carried his heavy bags over the threshold. They seemed fatuous too. Everything inside the entrance seemed very bright—the woman's smile, the gleam of mirrors and polished floorboards and brass and lustrous fabrics. "You're not carrying a candle," he said.

"Britain isn't that old-fashioned, Mr. Standish. You needn't have carried your bags by yourself, you know. The staff is here to make things easier for you. I'll get someone to take your things to your rooms straightaway, and you may go up to relax a bit after your journey. Then we shall see you in the dining room. Mr. Wall has been waiting for this moment." Now the beautiful smile was pure warmth again. "You must be famished, poor man."

Standish wondered if there was even the slightest chance that this woman might marry him.

"I take it there's nothing else in the car?"

She clearly expected him to say no. The light in her eyes informed him that he had brought too many clothes, and that she held out these two great straining bags to him as a joke she trusted him to share. He wished that the car and everything inside it would sink down into the drive and disappear.

"I guess I did bring a lot of stuff," he said. "I had to leave some things in the car."

"We'll fetch them up for you. We don't want you straining your back before you set to work."

She smiled as if in forgiveness of his inexperienced packing and turned away to lead him toward his rooms. Standish paused after a few steps. She hesitated and looked back at him. He gestured toward his ridiculously heavy suitcases, which sat like intruders in the polished entryway. "They'll be seen to," she said. "Everything will be seen to. You'll learn our ways, Mr. Standish."

He set off after her down the entry hall, which he now saw to be a screened passage lined with vast tapestries. Between the long tapestries he looked into a hall the size of a ballroom in which brightly upholstered furniture had been arranged before a tall stone fireplace with Ionic columns. Big gloomy paintings of huntsmen, children, and horses hung on the paneled walls. The next time Standish came to one of the openings between the screens, he saw a gallery running above the far side of the room. Curved wooden beams and arches overhung the gallery.

"That's the East Hall, the oldest part of the house," the woman said, looking back at him. "Elizabethan, of course."

"Oh, sure," Standish said.

They reached the end of the screened passage and turned left toward a staircase that seemed nearly as wide as the stairs in front of the house. Portraits of eighteenth-century noblemen glowed dully on either side of the staircase, which divided into two smaller, curving staircases at its top. Standish's guide began ascending the stairs, and he followed.

"I'm afraid there are more stairs, but you will be staying right above the library, in the Fountain Rooms. It's where we always put our scholarly guests, and they've always seemed quite comfortable there."

"Is there really a fountain?"

"In the courtyard, not in the room, Mr. Standish." Turning into the left branch of the staircase, she smiled again at him over her shoulder. "You have an excellent view of the courtyard from your rooms."

A question that had occurred to him in Zenith came to him now.

"Am I the only one? I mean, aren't there other people working in the library now?"

"No, of course not," she said, giving him a rather severe, questioning look and at last pausing to allow him to catch up with her. "I assumed you would have known. Excuse me. I seem to have forgotten that you've never been here before. We never invite more than one guest to make use of the library at any time. Scholarship seems a very individual activity, I suppose, and I think we always wanted our guests to be able to make full use of Esswood. Didn't want to have two people trying to use the same set of papers—your sort of work is actually very intimate, isn't it? Sharing it would be like sharing, oh, I don't know, a toothbrush or a bath towel or—"

A bed, Standish thought.

"Well," she said. Her eyes glowed. "At any rate, yes, you are the only one. You have three weeks in which all of Esswood, especially the papers in the library, is yours. In a manner of speaking."

"Do you think I might be able to get an extension for another week if it turns out I need it?"

"I should think it possible. We are nearly there now."

They were climbing the narrower side stairs together, and she smiled up at him.

"The Fountain Rooms are just ahead through the Inner Gallery. And the Inner Gallery is just beyond this—"

She opened a door at the top of the staircase and led him into a room or passageway that seemed as dark as a movie theater after the dazzle of his introduction to the house. About the size of the bedroom he shared with Jean back in Zenith, the dark room seemed crowded with furniture, uncomfortable, and cramped. "Lighting's wonky here. Must get it seen to. Study, this is, not used much now." In the gloom Standish picked out heavy chairs with ottomans, books in dim dull ranks on the walls. Shadowy and indistinct, the woman moved like a blur before his eyes, almost melting into the room, and threw open another door at its far end. She slipped through into a rectangle of yellow light.

Standish felt as though he were pursuing her.

He burst out into the next, brighter room half-expecting to see her moving ahead of him down a corridor. But she stood facing him from a point about six feet into a long high-ceilinged space too wide to be a corridor and too long and narrow to be a room. One side of this museumlike space was decorated with large paintings of horses and dogs and boats at sea, beneath which were arranged low uncomfortable-looking benches. The other side, Standish's left, was lined with a series of enormous windows that looked out onto the lighted windows of another vast house. Then Standish realized that the other house was another section of Esswood, and that he was looking out over the courtyard.

"Nearly there, Mr. Standish. This is the Inner Gallery, so called because there is another gallery, the West Gallery, on the second floor at the front of the house. The West Gallery was added in the seventeen thirties when Sir Walton Seneschal redid Esswood's facade in the Palladian style."

Palladian, Standish thought. That was the word he had not been able to remember. Then he remembered seeing the light, as of a flashlight or candle, passing behind the windows as he approached the house.

"The Gallery is on the second floor?" he asked.

"Both of them, yes."

"And the second floor is where I entered, at the top of the stairs?"

She stopped. "Why, no—you entered on the first floor. The one below is the ground floor. Americans always take a little time to learn our system." She began to move forward past the large dark windows.

Maybe he had been mistaken. "And you didn't carry a candle, or something like a candle, past the front windows when you heard me coming?"

She stopped again and looked up at him in a way that seemed almost tense with worry. Then her face softened. "Are you teasing me?"

And there it was again, the note of a subdued flirtatiousness just beneath the surface of her manner.

"I don't think I'd know how to tease you," Standish said.

The flirtatiousness disappeared so quickly that Standish wondered if he had imagined it. "I mean, I thought I saw someone carrying a lamp past the first-floor windows."

Her face smoothed out into a deliberate absence of expression. "I'm afraid that's not possible, Mr. Standish." She continued down the gallery a step ahead of him.

"And now we have arrived," she said, opening the door at the gallery's end. "Everything's been prepared for you. Your bags should be here in a moment. As soon as you're ready, Mr. Wall will be waiting in the dining room, which you can reach by returning to the ground floor, turning to the right of the main staircase, and going straight through the West Hall. Or you might take the back staircase from your room to the library, go past the library, and keep turning left in the corridor until you come to the double doors—that'll be the dining room."

"Fine."

She stepped back instead of leading him into the room, as he had hoped. To keep her from leaving, he said, "Are the Seneschals here now?"

She nodded. "They're seldom elsewhere. Miss Seneschal is an invalid and rarely leaves the family wing. Of course they're both quite old."

"They have no children?"

Her extraordinary face flickered, as if this time he really had gone too far, and she gestured toward the half-opened door to the Fountain Rooms. "Remember not to keep poor Mr. Wall waiting long—he'll be quite overcome with relief when he sees you. As overcome as you will be to see your dinner, I imagine."

"I look forward to seeing both of them. And to seeing you again, too." She shot what he took as a glance of humorous appreciation at him with her wide intelligent eyes, and she turned away.

Standish stepped through the door into the Fountain Rooms and turned to watch her walk away. He realized that she had never told him her name. He could not call out to her—he could not shout in Esswood. She opened the door at the far end of the gallery, and then she was gone.

His rooms were not what he had expected. The splendor of the rest of the house and the name, "Fountain Rooms," had led Standish to anticipate extravagance: gold and velvet, decorative antiques, a canopied bed. The reality of the Fountain Rooms was as mundane as a room in a slightly run-down old hotel.

It was a suite of two small rooms. The living room was furnished with stiff high-backed chairs and a couch covered in a floral chintz. A small table with ancient copies of *Country Life* and *The Tatler* stood before the couch. Standard lamps with big yellow shades shed mild light. A stuffed fox and a terrarium with dark green ferns stood on the mantel of the fireplace. Against a wall with rose-patterned paper there was a writing desk with a leather top and a green library lamp. A bookshelf beside the desk was crammed with novels by Warwick Deeping, Compton Mackenzie, John Buchan, and Agatha Christie. The books looked welded into place. On the pale walls with roses had been hung pictures of men in wigs and embroidered waistcoats playing cards in what looked like the East Hall downstairs, people in slightly more modern dress playing croquet on a terrace beneath the rear elevation of Esswood House, of a carriage drawn by prancing horses coming up the drive where Standish had left his car. A small spotted spaniel trotted alongside the carriage, his head raised. Through the windows on the left side of the room Standish saw the Seneschals' windows glowing back at him from across the courtyard. The room contained no television, radio, or telephone.

Slightly smaller than the living room, the bedroom was fitted with a narrow single bed with a bedside table and carved wooden headboard, a comfortable-looking wing-backed chair, a sofa covered with the same dark blue floral material as the bedspread, a second small desk, and a large wooden press for hanging clothes. Beside the press was a tall wooden door that must have led to the back staircase. There was another chest-high bookshelf, this one filled with what appeared to be a complete set of the writings of Winston Churchill. On the mantel of the bedroom fireplace was a pair of heavy ornate silver candlesticks, and above it hung a geometrical steel engraving that proved to be a plan of Esswood's terraces, showing a long pond, what appeared to be a little forest with a circular clearing like a druidical site, and fields. The shutters of the bedroom windows had been closed, and the entire room looked hazy in the low golden light of the lamps.

Standish pulled at the handles of a pair of mirrored doors, expecting to find a closet, and looked into a tiled bathroom. He stepped inside, closed the door behind him, and used the toilet. Afterward, he washed his hands and inspected his face in the mirror.

The rims of his eyelids showed a faint pink, like the eyes of a rabbit. Gray smears of dust lay across his cheeks. His receding hair, flat as seaweed, stuck to his head. Standish groaned. This was the face that the wonderful quick-witted woman had seen. What he had taken for flirtation had only been civilized pity. He had turned up hours late with an absurd amount of luggage, he had gaped like a tourist, he had undoubtedly leered. Yes, he had leered. Oh, God. Standish took off his jacket and unbuttoned his shirt. He filled the basin with hot water and washed his hands and face. Then he emptied and refilled the basin and quickly washed his hair.

He came out of the bathroom and saw his shirts, socks, and underwear laid out on the bed beside his bathroom kit. His four bags stood beside the bed. On the little desk was *Crack, Whack, and Wheel.* His suits and jackets and trousers had been hung in the press, his shoes arranged beneath them, his ties on a tie rack.

Standish put on a clean shirt, a new tie, and a blazer from the press. He changed his shoes for a pair of shiny loafers. The mirrored doors told him that he once again looked like a respectable young scholar. He felt light-headed with hunger, and decided that the back way to the dining room sounded faster than working his way through the gallery, the dark little study, and down the staircase. He marched up to the door beside the press and pulled it open.

four

On the other side was a bare unpolished wooden landing. A narrow flight of stairs dropped past a window and then curved out of sight. Low-wattage bulbs set in old gas fixtures gave the stairs a dim but even illumination. Standish moved across the landing and began to descend the stairs.

After the third or fourth turning of the staircase he looked back up the way he had come and saw only the smooth skin of the walls and the steep dark risers of the steps. He wondered if he had somehow missed the exit onto the first floor and was descending into the scullery, or the dungeon, or whatever they had in the basement here. Then he remembered the height of the hall with the enormous stone fireplace, and kept going downward. After another series of turns he came to a place where the light bulbs had burned out, and he continued down slowly, touching the walls on both sides. When the stairs turned again Standish expected to emerge into the light, but the darkness continued. He felt his way down another nine or ten steps in the dark. At another turn of the staircase, light from below began to wash the outer wall, and after another few steps he saw that his hands and the sleeves of his blazer were gray with spiderwebs.

A little while later he saw the bottom of the staircase beneath him. A flagged corridor illuminated by the same altered gas fittings led to a tall narrow door identical to the one in his bedroom. This must have been the door to the library. Standish came down the final few steps and went down the corridor to stand in front of the door. Almost guiltily he placed his hand on the brass doorknob. He looked sideways down the empty corridor. After all he had been through this day, no one would begrudge him a private treat. He had been invited to use the library: and Isobel had written a good deal of her verse on the other side of this door.

Standish turned the knob, so intent on seeing the library that when the door resisted him he turned it again and rattled it back and forth, as if he could force it open. Why was it locked? To keep the servants out? To keep *him* out? Standish remembered the dead lamps in the staircase, and wondered how long it had been since the last scholar had been invited to Esswood. Then he remembered what the publican in Huckstall had said about an American being murdered at Esswood, and quickly turned away from the door.

After about fifteen yards he came to a sharp left-hand turn in the corridor, marked by an Italianate marble statue of a small boy rising up on his toes, arms outstretched, as if for a kiss. Standish went past the statue into the new wing of the corridor and moved on in silence for another thirty or forty feet. Again there was an abrupt left-hand turn, this time into a wider, but still flagged and dimly lit corridor. At the turn, another marble statue, of a woman cowering back with her hands over her face, stood on a round marble-topped table. Now Standish could hear low voices and soft noises coming from somewhere within the house. At last he stood before a wide set of double doors. He knocked softly and saw dingy wisps of spiderwebs adhering to his cuff. He hastily wiped them off. No one answered his knock. Standish turned the knob, and heard a satisfying *thunk* as the lock withdrew into its stile. He pushed, and the thick door opened before him.

A man with a square sturdy face and thick gray hair that fell over his forehead blinked at him, then smiled and stood up on the far side of a long table that took up the middle of the room. A single place setting had been laid opposite him on the smooth white cloth. The man was several inches taller than Standish. "Ah, at last," he said. "Mr. Standish. How good it is to see you. I am Robert Wall."

As soon as Standish stepped forward he saw that the table was too wide for them to shake hands across it.

"Lost a bet with myself," Wall said. "You stick there, and I'll make the trek round."

Wall smiled at him with a touch of ruefulness and began to walk around the bottom of the table to greet him. He wore a beautifully cut gray tweed suit, a dark blue shirt, and a pink tie of raw silk. Wall was not quite what Standish had expected— he looked like a college president, not the administrator of an obscure literary foundation. His handsomeness struck Standish as an irrelevance, almost a hindrance. Wall marched up to him with his hand outstretched, and Standish realized how Jean would respond to the sight of this man.

"Allow me to welcome you properly," Wall said. He gave Standish a dry brisk handshake. "You *have* had a day of it, haven't you? Care for a drink before we have the opportunity of feeding you? Splash of whiskey? Single malt? Something special, I promise you."

Standish never drank whiskey, but heard himself agreeing. Up close, Robert Wall's face looked dusty with fatigue. Tiny wrinkles like razor cuts nicked the corners of his eyes and mouth. Wall grinned at Standish and turned away toward a pantry located behind a door at the bottom end of the table. Standish trailed after him. The size and splendor of the dining room both stimulated and oppressed him. Portraits of dead Seneschals frowned down from the walls, and wherever Standish looked he saw some unexpected ornamental detail: dental molding around the ceiling, the pattern of the parquet floor around the edges of the Oriental carpet, plaster rosettes around the light fixtures on the wall. The flatware set around his plate, and the plate itself as well as the rim of the wineglass beside it, were of gold. A golden plate! A golden fork, a golden spoon, a golden knife! The casualness of this opulence unsettled him, as if he had inadvertently stepped outside ordinary reality into the world of fairy tales.

Behind the glass-fronted cupboard doors in the pantry stood ranks of the golden plates, and in the cupboard at the far end was an array of bottles. A narrow staircase like the one Standish had taken from his room led downstairs, presumably to the kitchen. Robert Wall took a bottle from the shelf and two glasses from another cabinet.

"You said you lost a bet with yourself?"

"Yes, I did," Wall said, smiling at him as he passed back into the dining room. His obvious exhaustion and the tiny cuts around his eyes and mouth utterly negated his good looks when you were this close to him—he looked as though he were still recovering from a skin graft.

Then for an instant Standish thought that Robert Wall did not look exhausted or ill but simply hungry, like a man who has never ceased to long for the great prizes that he has seen hovering, all his life, just out of reach; like a man who has never given up wanting more than he has decided to settle for.

Wall eased past him in the narrow space of the pantry, and as both men emerged back into the dining room, Standish realized that it was he, not Wall, who was hungry—he was famished, ravenous as a starving wolf.

Carrying the bottle and the short glasses, Wall went up one side of the table, Standish the other. Wall gestured toward the place that had been set, and Standish sat.

"The bet was that you'd have taken the main staircase back downstairs, and come in here from the West Hall. You're very intrepid, finding your way by the back stairs."

Wall poured whiskey as he spoke. He leaned far over to pass Standish his glass, and then sank gracefully down into his own chair. For a moment filled with dismay, Standish found himself wondering if Wall were married to the woman who had shown him to his rooms.

Are you teasing me? For a moment he saw the woman's hawk-like face looking up at him.

"A woman showed me to my room," he said.

Wall nodded and raised his glass, giving Standish a look of vague disinterest. Standish took an experimental sip. The whiskey tasted like a rich smooth food. It was ambrosial. Wall was waiting for whatever he would say next. "The woman knew about the back staircase—that's how I knew about it. Who is she, by the way? She didn't tell me her name."

"Couldn't say. You're settled in all right?"

"Dark hair, very long and sort of *loose*? Extremely good-looking? About my age?"

"Mystery woman," Wall said. "You really are intrepid." He looked at his watch. "Your dinner should be ready in a moment. Just a question of warming it up. Do you like the malt?"

"Wonderful."

"Excellent—intrepid and blessed with good taste as well. It *is* rather special—seventy years old."

"You mean you don't know who she is?"

"I tend not to have much to do with that sort of thing. You had a peaceful journey?"

Standish described getting lost on the roundabout and miraculously finding his way to Huckstall, and the scene in the pub there.

"I was thinking afterward that the whole thing was like an Isobel Standish poem—an Isobel Standish kind of *experience,* if you see what I mean."

"A pity you should have chosen Huckstall for your first excursion into English life, but it can't be helped, can it?"

"Are they famous for waylaying visitors?"

"Not exactly. During dinner I'll spin you a tale." He glanced at his watch. "Where *is* your dinner? They should have brought it up by now. I expect they're waiting for us to finish our whiskey even as we wait for them to bring your meal." He stood up and went down the table and slipped through the pantry door. Standish heard him speaking to someone on the other side of the pantry door, then a low female laugh. Wall backed through the door with a tray in his hands. "Good job I didn't startle her into dropping this. They've given you a meal with a bit of a history. Loin of veal with morel sauce, some green beans too, I see. I'll open a nice bordeaux to go with that, shall I?"

Standish nodded. The smell of the food on the tray made him salivate. Wall set the plate down before him, and it fit perfectly into the larger golden plate. Wall carried the tray to the pantry, and reappeared instantly with a bottle of red wine and a corkscrew.

"I'll join you, if I may. We could continue our conversation until you want to go to bed. I must be off tomorrow afternoon, so I won't be here for a little time. Though I could have breakfast with you, if you like?"

"Please," Standish said, happy not to be abandoned to the dining room. He tried a small section of the veal, and a variety of tastes so subtle and powerful spilled into his mouth that he groaned out loud. He had never tasted anything even faintly like it. The cork came out of the bottle with a solid pop, and Wall poured deep red wine into his gold-rimmed glass. Standish swallowed, and the food continued to ring and chime in his mouth.

"You know why you're given veal with morels, of course?" Wall sat down on the other side of the table.

Standish shook his head. He continued to eat as Wall spoke, now and then pausing to sip the wine, which was as extraordinary as the food.

"Isobel Standish's favorite meal." Wall smiled at him. "When they heard that in the kitchen, there was no restraining them. We use fresh mushrooms, of course, and good veal can be had in the village. I'm happy you approve." He paused, and the benign expression on his face altered. "So you knew nothing of Huckstall before you stopped there? Its fame has not crossed the Atlantic?"

Standish shook his head. A circle of warmth in the center of his being was spreading outward millimeter by millimeter, bringing peace and contentment to every cell it touched.

"Little bit of trouble there, earlier this summer," Wall said. "Man killed his wife and her lover, then was killed himself. A publican."

Standish saw the stony, immobile face of The Duelists' proprietor vividly before him, and the wonderful food congealed on his tongue.

"Not much of a scandal by American standards, of course," Wall went on. "But it made quite a splash here. The woman was pregnant. The husband chained them up in the cellar of the pub and tortured them for several days. Finished up by decapitating both of them. The boyfriend was a prominent fellow locally, local poet, something of the sort. I didn't mean to spoil your meal, Mr. Standish."

"No, it's fascinating," Standish said. "It reminds me so much of the people I saw there."

Wall looked pleasantly bemused.

"In that pub, The Duelists."

"Ah." Wall smiled indulgently. "See what you mean. Can't remember the name of this fellow's pub at the moment. Lord

Somebody-Or-Other's, I think. Couldn't have been your place anyhow."

"Why not?"

"Chap burned it down after he committed the murders, didn't he? Completely off his head, of course. Excuse the pun, if that's what that was. Anyhow, he put the heads in grips of some sort and tossed them onto a slag heap. Probably thought that no one would ever find them. Or didn't care. His own life was useless to him anyway, wasn't it? He jumped in front of a speeding car just outside the village. Have some more of that wine, won't you?"

Standish saw with astonishment that his glass was empty. He lifted the bottle and poured. Wall pushed his own glass forward and Standish stood up to pour for him too.

"The impact killed him, but nobody discovered the body until the next morning—all busy fighting the fire, do you see? The pub went up like tinder. Danger the entire street might go up with it. And then of course after they'd put out the blaze they found the bodies, which had escaped most of the effects of the fire. Being in the cellar, you know. Oh!" His eyes flashed at Standish.

"I'd forgotten—the chap, the boyfriend fellow, wasn't the local poet. All part of the scandal. He *had* been important—not anymore. Fellow had been the librarian, something like that, headmaster perhaps, but had gone seriously downhill years before. Became a drunk. No job. Lived rough. Pub fellow couldn't take the humiliation of being cuckolded by a virtual tramp."

Standish ate steadily while Wall spoke, in reality now only half-tasting the wonderful food.

"This *is* a terrible tale for dinnertime, isn't it?"

"Not really," Standish said. "When I was in The Duelists—"

"I must tell you the rest. The next day, as I say, the body of the publican was found on the road. Man had been crushed by the car that struck him. Car was still there, you see—driver's door open, engine still running. No driver in sight. He had panicked and scarpered across the moor. Never knew he was innocent—never knew the whole tale."

"Didn't they track him through his car?"

"Rented. Fellow may have used a false name, as far as I know. He's still running, I suppose."

"The man in The Duelists told me that someone had been murdered here."

"At Esswood?"

"Yeah! An American, he said."

"That's very odd." Wall seemed entirely unperturbed. "I'm sure I should have heard of it. After all, I'm generally somewhere about the place." He was frowning-smiling, the frown being a disguise for a smile. It was perhaps the most ironic expression Standish had ever seen.

"I thought it sounded funny," Standish said.

"Can't really think when we last had a murder." Wall was nearly smiling outright. "And I've been around here most of my life. Your fellow had the name confused with Exmoor or something of the sort. You weren't worried about it, I hope?"

"Of course not. Not at all. Nope."

"You were clearly a good selection for an Esswood Fellowship, Mr. Standish."

"Thanks." Unsettled by the flattery, Standish wondered if he should ask Wall to call him William. Would Wall ask to be called Robert?

"Did you happen to peek into the library on your way through the back hallway? If I were in your shoes, don't think I could have resisted."

"Well, not really," Standish said, and Wall raised his eyebrows. "That is, to tell you the truth, I did try the door, but it was locked."

"I'm afraid that isn't possible. The library doors are never locked. Could it have been another door?"

"Near the bottom of the stairs?"

"Hmm. No matter. Sounds as if it didn't want to let you in. We may have to reconsider your application, Mr. Standish."

Now he knew he was being teased. He sipped his wine, and then met Wall's continuing silence with a question. "You said you've been at Esswood most of your life. Were you born here?"

"I was, in fact. My father was the gamekeeper before the first war, and we lived in a cottage beyond the far field." Wall poured for himself and Standish. "In those days, what drew guests here to Esswood was Edith Seneschal's hospitality and the fame of her kitchen, which as you see continues to be pretty good, but the pleasure they had in one another's company and whatever they found to enjoy in Esswood itself kept them coming back. Their gratitude for that pleasure led them to contribute to our library—which is of course why it is unique. Every literary guest we had donated manuscripts, papers, diaries, notebooks, drafts, material they knew to be significant as well as things they must have considered nearly worthless. Of course, some of the latter have turned out to be among our most important possessions."

"Manuscripts and diaries? T. S. Eliot and Lawrence and everybody else? Even Theodore Corn—even Isobel?"

"Oh, even Isobel, I assure you," Wall said, smiling. "Especially Isobel, I might say. I don't quite know how it began, but before long it had become a custom to give something of that sort to the house, as a token repayment for Edith's hospitality, as an indication of one's gratitude for Esswood's beauty and seclusion. . . . It was part of coming here at all, to leave something like that behind when you left."

"That's extraordinary," Standish said. "You mean that all these famous people donated original manuscripts and diaries every time they came?"

"Every year. Year after year. Isobel Standish came to Esswood twice, and I believe she left some very significant items for the library."

"And were these, um, donations, copies of more widely known works? It doesn't sound—"

"Nor should it. I *think* I'm right in saying that everything of that sort we have is unique to us. None of it can be published or reproduced elsewhere, except by arrangement. Those were the conditions that evolved, you see."

Standish felt as though he had licked his finger and pushed it into a socket. The place was a treasure house. Manuscripts of unknown works by some of the century's greatest writers, early handwritten drafts of famous poems and novels! It was like coming on a warehouse full of unknown paintings by Matisse, Cézanne, and Picasso.

Robert Wall must have seen some of his excitement in his face, for he said, "I know. Rather takes the breath away, doesn't it? If you're the sort of person who can appreciate it properly. Of course, you can see why we are very careful each year in selecting the Esswood Fellows—they have a great deal to live up to."

"Wow," Standish said. "Absolutely."

"And that was its attraction for me too, I imagine. Apart from its being the only home I've ever really known. I went to school and then university, the Seneschals were always very generous when they felt generosity was called for, but I'm afraid I always felt a deep connection to Esswood. So after university I did my best to make myself indispensable, and I've been here ever since. Called up in the second war, of course, but I couldn't wait to get back here. Still the gamekeeper's boy at heart, I fear. And I do like to think I've helped Esswood move into the modern world without losing anything of its past."

Wall smiled at Standish. "That's the thing, you see. The past of Esswood is really still quite alive. I can remember walking out past the long pond with my father one morning, and seeing Edith Seneschal, who seemed to me the loveliest woman in the world, wander toward me with a tall woman, also beautiful, and a stout, distinguished elderly gentleman, and introducing me to Virginia Woolf and Henry James. James was very old then, of course, and it was his last visit to Esswood. He bent down to shake my hand, and he admired my coat. 'What a lot of buttons you have, young man,' he said to me. 'Is your name Buttons?' I was tongue-tied, hadn't a clue what to say to him, just gawped up like a gormless fool, which he took awfully well. Later on in life, I read everything I could about them, James and Woolf, as well as all their work—I tried to learn everything possible about all our guests. Scholars included, of course. I see that as one of the essential tasks of running Esswood properly. We screen everybody pretty thoroughly beforehand, and try to get to know them even better while they're with us. We want to be well matched with our guests. It won't *work* as well as it should if it isn't a proper mating. The people who come here must love Esswood."

Standish nodded.

"But you see, I'm an advanced case. I love it so much I've never left."

"You're a lucky man."

"I agree. It's better never to leave Esswood."

Never to leave Esswood. Standish heard some unspoken message, a kind of silent resonance, in Wall's last words. Even Wall's posture, his head tipped back and his fingers wrapped around his glass, seemed to communicate the aura of an unspoken meaning. Then Standish realized at least one of the things Wall must have meant: he had been something like ten in 1914, and therefore must now be over eighty years old. The man looked to be somewhere in his fifties.

"Esswood has been good to you," he said.

Wall smiled slowly, and nodded in agreement. "Esswood and I try to be good to each other. I think it will be good to you too, Mr. Standish. We were all very happy when we received your application. Until then it looked as though there might not be an Esswood Fellow this year."

"I couldn't have been the only applicant!"

"No, we had about the usual number of applicants."

Standish raised his eyebrows in curiosity, and Wall indulged him. "Something over six hundred. Six hundred and thirty-nine, to be exact."

"And mine was the only one you considered?"

"Oh, you had some competition," Wall said. "There is always a period of several months while things sort themselves out. We do take what we consider to be more than usual care." He smiled with the same slow ease, and looked nothing like the son of a gamekeeper. "If you're finished, we could peek in at the library. Then I'll let you get the rest I'm sure you need. Unless you have some questions?"

Standish looked down at his plate. Most of the wonderful meal seemed to have consumed itself. "I guess I can't help wondering when I'll have the chance to meet the Seneschals."

Wall stood up. "They're not in the best of health."

"The woman who greeted me said that Mrs. Seneschal—"

Again Wall stopped him with a look that told him not to trespass.

"Let us try that troublesome door, shall we?"

Standish stood up. For a moment his head swam and he had to steady himself on the back of his chair. Some words that Robert Wall said to him vanished like everything else into gray fuzz, and then his head cleared and his vision returned. "Sorry."

"Do you feel all right?"

"Just a little spell. I missed what you said, I'm sorry."

Wall opened the door through which Standish had entered the dining room. "All I said was, you must have heard this mysterious person incorrectly. There is no Mrs. Seneschal."

Standish passed by Wall, and the deep grooves like scars in his face came into focus.

"It's Miss Seneschal. She and Mr. Seneschal are brother and sister. Edith's two surviving children."

"Oh, I was sure—"

"Simple mistake for a weary man."

Wall gestured down the length of the flagged corridor. "Unlike most of our guests on the first night, you already know this way quite well, don't you?" He set off in the direction by which Standish had come. "Yet another sign of our good judgment in selecting you."

They walked on a few paces, Wall striding like a youthful and well-exercised man.

"You're married, aren't you, Mr. Standish?"

They turned right at the statue of the woman shrinking back.

"Yes, I am."

"Children?"

"Not yet," Standish said, the skin at the back of his neck prickling. He thrust away from him the vision of a lighted window in a Popham apartment house, a drawn shade behind which two people, one of them a faithless wife and the other a faithless friend, clawed at one another in bed. Wall was looking at him inquisitively, and he added, "Jean is pregnant—expecting in two months."

"So we'd better get you home safe and sound before that, hadn't we?"

Standish nodded vaguely.

They turned right again, past the reaching boy.

"In any case, this is what you've come all this way to see. Let us try this puzzling door."

They stood before the tall narrow wooden door. Wall's face was a shadow beneath his handsome gray hair—entirely unwillingly, Standish saw Jean folding herself into Wall's arms, rubbing her face fiercely against his chest. Jean often made a fool of herself with handsome men.

"Seems to work normally." Wall turned his shadowy face toward Standish. "Perhaps you turned the knob the wrong way."

He had not turned the knob the wrong way. For an instant it was as if Jean, or her shade, had witnessed his humiliation, and Standish felt a ferocious blush leap across his face like a rash.

Wall stepped inside and flicked a switch. Warm bright light filled the doorway. "Come in, Mr. Standish."

Standish followed him into an enormous room which seemed at first to contain a disappointingly small number of books. Most of the room consisted of vast empty space. Bright white Corinthian columns shining with gold leaf at top and bottom stood before curved recesses ranked with books. Books spanned the library beneath classical murals. Almost immediately he realized that there were thousands and thousands of books, books on shelves all around the massive room, books reaching nearly to the barrel-vaulted ceiling as ornate as a Wedgwood china pattern, books and manuscript boxes everywhere, in every molded, flowing section of the huge room. Chairs and chaises of red plush with gilded arms stood at intervals alone the walls, and a massive chair sat before a wooden writing desk in the middle of the room, on the center rosette of a vast peach-colored Oriental carpet. Over the mantel of the marble fireplace on the left side of the library hung a large portrait of a gentleman in eighteenth-century clothes and white wig looking up from a folio propped on the library's writing desk. The library's walls, and the section of the high-vaulted ceiling not covered with ornate plaster palmettes, husks, arabesques, and scrolls, were painted a cool, almost edible color hovering between green and gray that seemed lit from within. The entire space of the library was filled with radiant light that came from no visible source. Standish had spent much of his life in libraries without seeing one like this. He wondered if he really could walk through it—it seemed too good to use, like some delicate clockwork toy or Fabergé egg.

"Rather good, isn't it?" Robert Wall was leaning back against one of the pillars, his arms crossed over his chest. "It's a Robert Adam room, of course. One of his most successful, we think."

"What are those columns made of? I thought they were painted, but—"

"Alabaster. Striking, isn't it? As good as anything at Saltram House. They look freshly painted until you see those delicate veins in the stone." In his ambiguous face was a full understanding of just what Standish was feeling.

Wall pushed himself forward and stood up. "Now I must take you through the main entrance and point you up the staircase. It's a little late to creep through the servants' corridor. Though I daresay in the old days the servants' corridor saw a great deal of surreptitious movement."

Standish smiled before he understood what Wall meant. Wall led him out through an archway set between two of the alabaster columns, then through a pair of ornately carved wooden doors and into another high vast room that seemed cold and museumlike after the library.

Before them, across an expanse of dark carpet and through the middle of a double row of stiff chairs like soldiers, was another set of carved doors.

"Dining room can be reached through there," Wall said, indicating the far doors, "and the main staircase which takes you up to the Inner Gallery and the Fountain Rooms is directly ahead of you. Until we meet again, then. We will see to your car tomorrow. Don't give it a thought.

The two men began to move down past the soldierly chairs.

"I can't help but wonder what happens to the place once Edith's children die. Who inherits the place?"

"I'm afraid there's no proper answer to that."

"What does that mean? That you can't tell me?"

Instead of answering, Wall opened the door at the far end of the uncomfortable room, and stood waiting for Standish to go through. For a moment he reminded Standish of the landlord of The Duelists.

"I'm sorry if that was an awkward question."

"I'm sorry if you didn't like my answer. But if you want to know anything else, ask away. You may have three questions."

"Well, I guess I'm curious about Isobel. I mean I know she died here, and I guess I always assumed that she had some illness. Do you remember anything about it?"

Wall continued to hold the door and look down at Standish. His expression had not changed in any way.

"Did she have influenza?"

"Is that your second question?"

"Well, I know there were influenza epidemics around then. . . . Do you remember Isobel at all? I've never even seen a picture of her."

"That is your third question. Of course I remember Isobel. It was a great loss for all of us when she died. Everyone here cared for her deeply." He motioned Standish through the door, and followed him out into the great hall. "She died in childbirth, to answer your real question. I'm rather surprised that you should not have known."

"I didn't even know that she'd had a child," Standish said.

"The child died too." Wall smiled and stepped away. "You do remember how to get back to the Fountain Rooms?"

When Standish reached the top of the wide staircase he turned to look back down at Robert Wall, but the entire first floor of Esswood was dark. He heard a burst of female laughter from beneath him, as if it had risen up the stairs like smoke.

In the bedroom he undressed and discovered that the sheets were delightfully cool and the bed just as firm as he liked a bed to be. He heard the lights in the Inner Gallery click off. Far away a door closed softly.

five

S tandish and a number of other men were being held captive in a large bare cabin with a plank floor and rough wooden walls. Armed guards in brown uniforms lounged against the walls, idly watching the prisoners and speaking to one another in low unintelligible voices. At one end of the huge wooden room was a low raised platform where a man whose gray hair had been shaved close to his bullet head sat behind a desk. Stacks of pages lay on the surface of the desk, and the man examined papers one by one before transferring them from one stack to another. He was dressed in a baggy gray suit and a wide florid necktie, and the points of his shirt collar turned up. Like the uniformed guards, he looked bored. The faces of all the men, the guards and the official behind the desk, were broad, fleshy, masculine, roughened by alcohol and comfortable with brutality and death. Through windows cut into the sides of the building Standish saw snow falling steadily onto a white landscape. At irregular intervals a man holding a rifle and bundled into a heavy dark coat and a fur cap struggled past the windows, gripping the leashes of two straining dogs. All of these men were at ease with the cold and the perpetual snow. They were at ease with everything they did. The atmosphere was of unhurried bureaucratic peace.

Fearful, Standish stood in the middle of the room with the other captives. All but he wore colorless woolen garments that resembled pajamas. Standish knew that in time he too would be stripped of his jacket, shirt, tie, trousers, and shoes, and be dressed in the woolen pajamas. There was no possibility of escape. If he managed to get outside and evade the guards and the dogs he would die of exposure.

The shoulders of his fellow prisoners were bent, their heads cropped, their faces shadowy. They had reconciled themselves to death; in a sense they were already dead, for nothing could move or touch them, nothing could jar them out of their apathy.

Standish experienced the purest dread of his life.

The man at the desk was selecting the order in which Standish and his fellow prisoners were to be executed. There was no possibility of pardon. Sooner or later this bored extermination machine was going to snuff out each one of them. There was nothing personal about it. It was business: a matter of moving papers from one stack to another.

The man at the desk looked up and uttered a monosyllable. One of the guards straightened up, walked toward the group of prisoners, and seized one man by the elbow. The prisoner got to his feet and allowed himself to be pulled toward the door. Nobody but Standish watched this. The guard opened the door and handed the prisoner almost gently to a man in a dark coat and fur hat. This second guard pulled the prisoner away into the snow, and the door closed.

Standish knew that the prisoner was going to be beheaded. Somewhere out of his range of vision was a wooden chopping block and a basket that caught the severed heads.

He glanced toward the door, and knew that one of the guards would shoot him if he even touched the knob.

Standish paced around the middle of the room under the eye of the guards. Some of the other prisoners were also walking aimlessly around the room, and Standish avoided looking at them closely. Some of the men sat on the floor, their backs bowed, and some curled up on the planks as if asleep, hiding their faces in their hands. Standish did not want to see their faces. If you saw one of the faces—

—then you saw it tumbling off the block, its eyes and mouth open, the brain still conscious, still recording and reacting to the shock, the terrible knowledge . . .

Standish realized that he was not dreaming. Somehow he had ventured into this wretched country, been captured, condemned to death, and transported to this penal outpost with these degraded men. He looked wildly around, and the two nearest guards watched him closely. Standish forced himself to walk slowly up to one of the cabin's walls. He placed his hand on the cold wall. A swift continuous draft flowed into the room from the gaps between the boards.

The official called out another name, and in the blur of sound Standish heard *st* and *sh*. His blood thinned. A languid guard pushed himself off a wall and walked toward him. Standish could not move. The guard advanced, looking at him expressionlessly. Standish opened his mouth and found that he could not form words. He saw large black pores on the guard's stony face and a long white scar, puckered like a vertical kiss, running from his right eye to the middle of his cheek.

The guard brushed past Standish and grasped the upper arm of a man in gray pajamas just behind him. The guard began to jerk the man toward the door. As they passed Standish, the prisoner lifted his head and looked directly into Standish's face. His eyes were black and flat as stones. Standish stepped backward, and the guard pulled his prisoner away.

Standish turned around and saw a baby lying on a blanket that had been folded on a small table against the opposite wall. The baby jerked its hands toward its face, then froze. The baby's hands drifted down to its sides as slowly as if the baby were underwater. It was a new baby, red-faced, only a few days old. It wore coarse woolen baby clothes of the same material as the prisoners' pajamas. The baby seemed to gasp for air. Standish took a step forward, and the baby's arms jerked spasmodically toward its head. Puffy, swollen-looking pads of flesh covered the baby's eyes.

One of the guards shouted at Standish, who stopped moving and pointed at the baby. "I want to pick it up. What can be wrong with that?"

The man behind the desk carefully placed the paper in his hand down on a neutral space on his desk and uttered a short series of monosyllables that caused the soldier to lower his rifle and retreat to the wall. Standish swallowed.

The official turned his head to look at Standish. His eyes were the color of rainwater in a barrel. "This not your baby," the official said in a slow, heavily accented voice. "Possible you understand? This baby not your baby."

And then Standish understood that he had lost everything. He was to be beheaded in this ugly country, and the baby gasping on the table was not his baby. Black steam filled his veins. He groaned, at the end of his life, and woke up in a sunny bedroom at Esswood.

six

"Got it wrong again," said Robert Wall. It was half an hour later. Carrying two pencils, a legal pad, and his copy of *Crack, Whack, and Wheel*, Standish closed the door from the servants' corridor and came near the table. Two places had been set. Golden domes with handles covered the plates. "You are indeed a fellow who prefers the less-traveled road, Mr. Standish."

"I guess I am," Standish said.

"As your tastes in literature would indicate. Let us see what is beneath these covers, shall we?"

They raised the golden domes. On Standish's plate lay an entire dried-out fish with bulging eyes.

"Ah, kippers," Wall said. "You're a lucky fellow, Mr. Standish. We're a bit shorthanded here just now, in fact I'm off to Sleaford in an hour or so to interview some prospective help, and you can never be sure what they'll serve up at breakfast. Last week I had porridge four days running."

Standish waited until Wall had separated a section of brown flesh from the kipper's side, exposing a row of neat tiny bones like the bars of a marimba, and inserted it in his mouth. When he tried to do the same, bristling bones stabbed his tongue and the inside of his cheeks. The fish tasted like burned mud. He chewed, glumly tried to swallow, and could not. His throat refused to accept the horrible wad of stuff in his mouth. Standish raised his napkin to his mouth and spat out the bony mess.

"And now," Wall was saying, lifting the cover from a dish that stood between them. Standish prayed for real food— scrambled eggs, toast, bacon.

"This *is* good luck," Wall said, exposing a pasty yellow-white partially liquefied substance. "Kedgeree." He began loading it enthusiastically onto his plate. "An aquatic morning, this. Do help yourself."

"Do you suppose there's any toast around here?" Standish said.

"Beside your plate." Wall gave him a surprised look. "Under the toast cover."

He had not even seen the second, more elongated golden lid next to his plate. He lifted it off and uncovered a double row of brown toast in a metal rack. Between the rows of toast stood a pot of orange marmalade and another of what looked like strawberry jam, each with a golden spoon. Standish ladled marmalade onto a wedge of toast.

"Something amiss with your kipper?"

"Wonderful, great," Standish said.

"I hope you had a comfortable night?"

"Fine."

"No trouble sleeping? No discomfort of any kind?"

"Nothing."

"Very good." Wall paused, and Standish looked up from smearing jam on another triangular wedge of toast. "There is one matter I must discuss with you. It's of minor importance, I'm sure, but I didn't want to bring it up last night."

"Oh?" Standish held the jam spoon in one hand, the triangle of toast in the other.

"There seems to be some confusion about the circumstances under which you left your first teaching position. Popham College, was it?"

Standish looked at him in an excellent imitation of genuine wonderment. "Confusion?" After a bit he looked down at the objects in his hands. Thoughtfully he applied jam to the toast.

"Certainly nothing that should cause you concern, Mr. Standish, for if it were you would not be here today. But—well, I don't think I am betraying confidences if I say that we had intimations of a conflict of some kind, though nothing ever seemed positively worrisome to us."

"Popham was a very small college," Standish said. His underarms had become damp. "A small college is like a small town. Especially the English Department of a small college. There's an unbelievable amount of gossip. In fact, when I arrived, people were still talking about something that had happened thirty years earlier between a student and an English professor named Chester—"

"I see," Wall said, smiling at him.

"What happened was really very simple." He closed his eyes and remembered how Jean had struggled on the steps to the ordinary little house in Iola, Popham's larger neighbor, how she had given up on the doorstep when the nurse who was not a nurse had opened the door, how the purity of his hatred had moved him through days when sorrow or love would have killed him. "I saw things clearly," he said, and cleared his throat. "A little more clearly than most of the other people on the faculty. It was obvious that most people in my department resented me. One man in particular, a false friend, behaved unspeakably. You could use the word betrayal. There was no unpleasantness, of course—"

"No," said Wall.

"—but it just sort of became clearer and clearer that Popham and William Standish were not made for each other."

"They were jealous of you?"

"Right. After a while we all understood that I'd be happier elsewhere. I think I'm still trying to find the right place for me. Zenith is all right, but I can't spend the rest of my life there."

Wall now looked embarrassed to have brought the matter up. "Yes, I see," he said, deftly separating the smoked fish's flesh from its picket-like bones. For a time the two men ate their separate meals in silence. When Standish glanced up and caught Wall staring at him, he instantly dropped his eyes.

"Yes," Wall said. "Well, it's of no real importance."

"I don't see how it could be." Standish felt a flash of hot impatience, another flash of memory too—of standing on a summery street swaddled in a Burberry and hat, looking up at a shaded window on the worst day of his life. "I could say a lot more, you know, but I don't think—"

"Nor do I," Wall said, and the two men finished their breakfasts in a silence Standish attributed to the other man's tact.

"So today you begin," Wall said as they pushed themselves away from the table.

They walked side by side through the great rooms.

Wall opened the library doors and for a moment both men stood mutely in the entrance. Like Standish's bedroom, the library was filled with morning light. The brightness and splendor of the gold trim on the pillars and the furniture seemed utterly fresh in the sunlight, and the long carpet glowed. Standish heard himself sigh.

"I know," Wall said. "I feel that way every time I see it."

Through a window set between bookcases at the library's far end, Standish could see Esswood's terraces falling away into a hazy green distance. Stands of trees that might have been painted by Constable bent toward the pond at the bottom of the terraces. Everything, grass, trees, and pond, looked as if it had just been born. A windmill revolved in slow motion atop a distant hill.

"Isobel's never really been taken seriously before," Wall said. "You're convinced, are you, that she was a poet of the first rank? She was something other than a normal guest, you know."

Standish turned to face him, and the taller man edged sideways.

"Perhaps it's the wrong time for this discussion," Wall said. "Let me show you where the Isobel Standish material is kept."

Standish was surprised by the extent of his desire to be left alone. Wall had insulted him twice, obscurely, and with ironic English good manners.

"It's in the first recess, straight through and on the right." He hesitated, as if puzzled by Standish's sudden diffidence. The "hungry" look was very clear on his face. "Well. I suppose there's nothing left to do but wish you luck in your research."

Standish thanked him.

"I'll leave you to it, then."

"Fine, good, okay."

Wall seemed to decide not to say something that came into his mind. He nodded and walked away with what seemed a deliberate lack of hurry.

Standish walked around the great room, trying to familiarize himself with the library as a whole. He peeked into the recesses but did not leave the central room until he thought he understood its basic organization.

The Seneschals had laid down their library in almost geological layers. The first serious accumulation of books seemed to begin in the seventeenth century, with a strong preponderance toward religion. Shelf after shelf had been filled with theology, the Patristic writings in huge leather folios, Greek and Latin commentaries, and church histories. Bound volumes of sermons filled two shelves. In the eighteenth century, the focus of the collection shifted toward politics, geography, and natural history. The only items of literary interest amongst the volumes concerning Antipodean Flora and Parliamentary papers were complete collections of *The Spectator,* Johnson and Boswell, as well as various editions of Shakespeare, Marlowe, and other Elizabethan dramatists. In the nineteenth century Esswood's library had nearly doubled in size, and for the first time became primarily concentrated on literature. Standish idled past books by Dickens from *Sketches by Boz* to *The Mystery of Edwin Drood* in the part-numbers in which some of them had first appeared, in individual volumes, and in bound sets; past complete collections of Trollope, Thackeray, Wilkie Collins, Cardinal Newman, Tennyson, Keats, Shelley, Matthew Arnold, Browning, Mrs. Gaskell, and the Brontë sisters; past ranks of *The Cornhill* in brown leather bindings; and Swinburne and Dowson and Oscar Wilde; and Henry James—an astonishing amount of Henry James, which took Standish up to the twentieth-century collection.

Edith Seneschal took over around the time of *The Ambassadors,* Standish reckoned, and continued as the main force behind the library until a few years after the publication of *The Wasteland* and *Ulysses.* Everything in between, Georgians, Edwardians, Vorticists, Imagists, Futurists, War poets and Modernists, in little magazines, broadsides, pamphlets, chapbooks, every sort of publication possible, was represented as only a passionate collector could manage it. The approximately thirty-five years of Edith's reign occupied as much shelf space as the whole of the nineteenth century. Afterward, the collection dwindled away to a few almost randomly selected novels—on the library's last shelves, looking far too contemporary and almost out of place, were books by Auden, Spender, MacNeice,

Isherwood, E. F. Benson. P. G. Wodehouse, Waugh, Kingsley Amis. The last few books, thrust in almost carelessly, were *Lunch Poems, The Tennis Court Oath,* and *Anglo-Saxon Attitudes.* The Seneschal children had never seriously tried to augment the Esswood library in the way their ancestors had.

Standish felt a pure and uncomplicated longing to be like Robert Wall. He yearned to live in this place, unencumbered by any other attachments, forever.

Maybe he could become Robert Wall. Someone had to care for the library after Wall's death. Why not a dedicated young American scholar?

Robert Wall was aptly named: he *was* a wall.

Standish walked to the window and looked down over the pond to the fields. The sun had grown higher. Everything before Standish was drenched in warmth and suffused with a relaxed quiet accumulating energy. A woman in a long dress of a pale green stood down at the bottom of the terraces on the far side of the long pond. She must have just emerged from the trees. Her face was a white smudge. Standish saw tension in her posture and the set of her legs and realized that she was angry or distressed. She turned from the house and began to pace down the length of the pond. In a moment she had vanished beneath the final terrace.

Standish leaned forward and touched his forehead against the glass. The woman did not reappear. He supposed that she must have been old Miss Seneschal.

He left the window and walked between two columns to the first recess.

It was a wide alcove stacked with bookshelves on both sides. The vaulted ceiling in the recess was patterned with plaster pineapples, candlesticks, and scrolls. Soft even light filled the recess, illuminating the curved backs of brown, green, and yellow boxes made from leather and thick board. Each of these boxes was stamped in gold with a single name.

For a moment Standish felt almost reverent.

The names stood like golden statuettes before the material hidden in the boxes. Everything in the boxes was alive because it had not been brought out to dry and harden in the air: what was contained in the boxes stayed alive because it was secret.

For a second he saw Wall's shadowy figure poised over an open file box, his face dripping red.

Then at the end of the third shelf on the right-hand side of the recess he saw his own last name stamped on three of the fat file boxes. He went up to the boxes stamped *Standish* and touched the first of them. It was of sturdy dark green ridged board.

Standish slid the box, heavy as a carton of bricks, off the shelf.

He set the box down on top of the desk in the center of the library. Standish lowered himself into the chair and tilted his head and looked up. In the central panel of the vault, surrounded by an oval of ornate white plaster, a stern bearded god leaned out of a whirling storm and leveled his index finger at Standish. Standish swallowed.

He bent forward and sprung the catch to open the box. Loose sheets of paper immediately spilled out onto the desk. Tiny, impenetrable black handwriting, Isobel's, covered the pages. Standish's heart began to thump. His trembling hands caused another waterfall of papers from the box.

Standish peered at a dense page. Many words and lines had been crossed out, and every inch of the margins had been covered with additions and second thoughts. To Standish it looked very like a page from a manuscript of a novel. In the top right-hand margin, encircled by scribbled words, was the number 142. Standish deciphered the words *I, project, impossible.* Another set of squiggles resolved themselves into *immortality.*

Just for a moment Standish felt as if an invisible hand had seized his heart and given it a light but palpable squeeze.

It is cruel, he read at the bottom of the page. The words that followed leaped into legibility. *It is cruel, this bargain we make with the Land. Too cruel, but is not eternity cruel, and immortality, and art? Once chosen, you cannot refuse.* Then the writing again dissolved into hieroglyphs and squiggles.

He grunted and heaved the eighty-pound box from the desk and deposited it on the floor. He reached in and removed a thick handful of papers.

The box contained as many as eight hundred loose pages and one manila folder. Standish removed the folder and opened it. The top page bore the initials B.P. Beneath them Isobel had written her own initials. The next page was numbered 65, and was no clearer than the other densely scrawled pages in the box.

Standish sorted through the papers until his stomach growled. Afternoon light filled the library. He looked at his watch and found that it was nearly two. He was hungry again. Samples of Isobel's tiny crowded writing lay across the desk like fragments of one great sentence fallen from the sky, dropped perhaps by the irritated god—with his frown and his pointing finger he was telling Standish to put all that stuff back together again.

In the dining room, a golden cover kept a golden plate warm. Golden utensils were placed beside it. A bottle of wine stood in a golden ice bucket filled with cold water and floating chips of ice. Esswood's invisible servants had declared him a wine drinker. Standish pulled the dripping bottle halfway out of the bucket. Puligny Montrachet, 1972. Presumably that was okay stuff. He raised the cover from the plate and found beneath it, as fragrant as the night before, slices of a loin of veal with morel sauce.

Standish sat down and saw a note beneath the wineglass.

> *Mr. Standish, I may be away from Esswood longer than anticipated. If you find that you require anything in my absence simply leave a note listing your requirements outside the library door. Other guests have found that this arrangement permits them to work undisturbed.*
>
> *Luncheon will be served at approximately one o'clock and dinner is generally around eight.*
>
> *Until my return, RW*

After lunch Standish took "his" corridor back to the library and returned to his desk. He felt heavy and slow, but pleasantly numb. Impulsively, he wrote *box of paper clips, 3 ballpoint pens, 3 manila folders, 3 notebooks* on a sheet of legal paper, tore off the sheet, and carried it through the alabaster pillars to the entrance. He opened the door and set the long yellow sheet on the carpet.

Back at his desk, he opened the folder and riffled through forty or fifty pages of *B.P.* The numbers were out of sequence; some pages had no numbers at all. Standish yawned, then amazed himself by farting hugely. The eighteenth-century Seneschal frowned down at him, the dyspeptic god threw a thunderbolt, and Standish fell into sleep as a stone falls down a well.

Some time later he came to with a pounding in his head and an ache in his bladder. His mouth tasted like a sewer. He stood up shakily, and the stack of papers in the file spilled out of his lap onto the floor. He groaned and bent down to stuff them back into the file. He stood up and moved away from the desk. Now he had a clear view of the window. The shadows of the gnarled trees slanted toward the fields. His watch said that it was four-thirty. Then there was a movement near the trees, and Standish ignored his bladder long enough to move closer to the window. A woman in a soft close-fitting hat and a long pale dress had come out of the trees near the long pond. Around her the hedges and fields sizzled with that same irrational bursting energy he had sensed earlier. The woman took a step forward, then hesitated and turned around. She looked as if she were arguing with someone who stood hidden in the trees. She looked up at Standish's window, and he moved back even before he realized that he was frightened. Still holding the folder, he let himself out into the servants' corridor.

A huge spiderweb he had broken on his first night fluttered and rippled as he passed through it, sending out loose gray tendrils like fingers. At last Standish burst into his room, grimacing with effort and already unbuckling his belt. He got to the toilet just in time. Panting, he leaned backward and saw the folder on the shelf behind the tub, where he had dropped it. He picked it up and opened it.

B.P., he thought. He ripped toilet paper from the roll.

The Birth of the Poet.

That was it—Standish felt as if he had heard it spoken in Isobel's own voice. She had written an account of her experiences at Esswood and donated it with the rest of her papers.

As he washed his hands he decided to read the memoir at night. It would be an invaluable backdrop to the poems. Then it seemed to him that the memoir too ought to be publishable. He foresaw another lengthy introduction, another crucial book. *Isobel Standish at Esswood: A Poet at the Crossroads.*

Standish trotted down the curving staircase.

This discovery meant that he would need much more than three weeks at Esswood. It would take another month to work his way through the hundreds of pages of Isobel's handwriting. At the same time, he had to conduct a thorough investigation of her poetry. He wondered if Wall would give him another month. If he presented a well-argued case that alluded to the advantages to Esswood itself in publicizing Isobel's account of her productive time here . . . And Jean would forgive him taking the extra time as long as he got back before she gave birth. A small, almost invisible flare of anger and humiliation went off in his chest at the thought of his wife. He imagined fat Jean squatting to give birth: blood and gore flopping out of her along with the child. Standish shook his hand at the flapping tendrils of the spiderweb, dismissing these feelings as well as whatever lay behind them—he had no time now for destructive emotions. The stairs wound around and around, going farther and farther down, far past the point where he thought they ended. At length he reached the bottom of the stairs and rushed the short distance down the corridor and let himself in.

He nearly sighed with pleasure. The desk was heaped with papers, the columns stood guard, the beautiful rows of books lined the walls. The portrait commanded him to sit and work. Then he remembered Wall's note and his response to it, and turned to the main entrance.

In a straight line on the carpet outside the doors, arranged like the corpses of mice brought in by a loving cat, were a box of number-one paper clips, three yellow Bic pens, three stenographic notebooks, and three manila folders.

seven

T he low sun was still visible when Standish had finished
separating what appeared to be drafts of poems from the
far more numerous pages of prose. The next day he could sort
through the second box, and if he had time, begin to divide the
pages of poetry into published and unpublished; after dinner
tonight he could begin paginating and reading the memoir.

There was an hour before dinner. He decided to walk down
the terraces and enjoy the hazy light and long shadows.

At the end of the screened passage he let himself out onto
the wide terrace at the top of the marble stairs and inhaled air
so sweet and heavy with fragrance that it was like a drug. No
wonder literary Londoners had so readily trekked to Beaswick:

after the smoky London of the early twentieth century, Esswood would have seemed a paradise. Standish went down the steps, his knees stiff from the day behind his desk. Four steps from the bottom he looked back up at the house. *Americans always take a little time to learn our system.*

And: *Are you teasing me?*

Ah, a joke within a joke.

It struck him that the house looked empty. The servants were somewhere inside, old Miss Seneschal and old Mr. Seneschal must have been pottering around inside the East Wing, but that side too looked abandoned. A reflected cloud scudded past a row of third-floor windows.

At the bottom of the steps he walked across the crunchy gravel to the right side of the house.

Large smooth flagstones ran beneath the arch of the trellis, which was densely grown with thick green vines and broad dark leaves. Halfway down the side of the house, the trellis parted around a low wooden door. At its far end he emerged again into bright sunlight and saw the land falling away before him in three broad terraces to the long dark pond. This was bordered at either end by the stands of gnarled, leaning trees from which the woman in green had emerged. A steep metal staircase, painted black, ran down the slope of the terraces.

He moved toward the staircase. Far away, on the other side of the long pond and a little forest, a wide field striped by a mower sloped upward to a row of straight feathery trees that served as the border of another, higher field. White sheep like dots of wool stood so motionless they looked painted. At the top of the far field the blades of a windmill shaped like a beehive turned slowly in a drifting breeze.

An unchanging paradise would have such fields, such ponds and trees, even the unmoving sheep and the drowsy windmill. It came to him that he was wholly happy for the first time since boyhood.

The black paint on the iron railing was flaky and pitted with rust. The entire structure clanged when Standish moved onto the first step. He grasped the gritty railing and looked back at the house.

From the rear the building had the massivity of a prison. The rough stone facing of the ground floor gave way to undistinguished brick. The windows at the back of the house were uniformly smaller than those at the front. Here and there blackened timbers, relics of some earlier Esswood, were visible within the brickwork. Only the library windows were not curtained.

Standish began to move down the iron staircase.

White iron lawn chairs and a sturdy iron table had been set out on the first terrace. The second was a smooth green swatch of lawn, oddly blank, like an empty stage.

When he reached the bottom of the stairs his palm was stained orange from the rust. Behind him the staircase chimed and vibrated against the bolts.

Over the tops of the trees Standish could see the feathery trees and the field topped by the windmill. A thick, buttery odor hung in the air—an almost sexual smell of grass, water, and sunlight. It occurred to Standish that this was a perfect moment: he had been inhabiting a perfect moment since he had come out from under the trellis. He walked across a track of crushed red gravel and bent to immerse his hand in the pond. The water met his flesh with a cold live shock that refreshed his entire body. Had they swum here, Isobel and

Theodore Corn and the others? He swirled his hand gently in the water, watching the rust deposit drift away like a cloud of orange blood.

Shaking his right hand, he stood up and turned toward the house. From the pond it looked less ugly, more like the prosperous merchant-landowner's house it had been before Edith had turned it into a sort of art colony.

An enormous butterfly with deep, almost translucent purple wings like fragments of a stained-glass window bobbled in the heavy air over the pond, and Standish's breath caught in his chest as he watched it zigzag upward with aimless grace. Its angle to the light altered, and the thick wings became a dusty noncolor. Then Standish half-saw, half-sensed a movement in the house, and he looked up the terraces and saw a figure standing in the library window. A smudge of face above a blur of green hovered behind the glass. His viscera went cold. The woman was shouting at him: a black hole that must have been her mouth opened and closed like a valve. He had a sense of anger leaping like a flame. The pale blobs of her fists flattened against the glass. With a rush of panic, he remembered driving north on the motorway and seeing the child shut up in the red brick house: it was as if she had pursued him here, still demanding release.

Standish put his hand on his chest and breathed hard for a moment, then began to move around the pond toward the house. The woman stepped back from the window and disappeared. Red dust lifted from the stones each time he took a step.

eight

At five minutes to eight he backed awkwardly into the dining room through the door from the secret corridor. Cradled in his arms were two bulky folders, one filled with drafts of poems, the other with partially ordered pages of *The Birth of the Poet*. He planned to go through the poetry while he ate, and to make a sustained effort at reading the memoir in the Fountain Rooms after dinner.

When he turned around he saw his place laid in the now-familiar manner: the golden tableware, the domed covers, and the gold-rimmed wineglass. An opened bottle of red burgundy stood beside the glass. Two candles burned in golden candlesticks.

He put the files on the table and sat down. He placed his hand over the cover. He hesitated for a second, then lifted the cover and looked down at slices of veal loin covered with a brownish sauce and morel mushrooms. "Now wait a second," Standish said to himself. He replaced the cover.

He saw the face of the marvelous woman who had let him into Esswood looking back up at him over her shoulder. There were two women in the house—one, old Miss Seneschal, who distrusted him and peered at him through windows; and the other, who teased. He stood up and went into the butler's pantry.

"What are you trying to do, fatten me up for the kill?" he called out.

A burst of giggles floated toward him from the kitchen.

An even diffuse light, like soft light in the library, filled the narrow stairwell. Standish trotted down to a bend in the staircase, around a half-landing, down again. He felt a bubble of elation rising to his throat from the center of his life, deep deep within.

"You have to eat this stuff with me, at least," he called, and came down into the kitchen.

A row of old iron sinks stood against one bright white wall, an electric dishwasher and a long, dark green marble counter beside them. White cabinets hung on the wall. On the opposite side of the room was a huge gray gas range with two ovens, a griddle, and eight burners. In the middle of the room was a large work surface covered with the same green marble. A golden corkscrew with handles like wings lay on the marble.

"Hey!" Standish shouted. "Where are you? Where'd you go?"

Laughing, he threw out his arms and turned around. "Come on!"

She did not answer.

His laughter drained away. "Aw, come on," he said. He peeked around the side of the big counter. "Come on out!"

Standish walked all the way around the divider and touched the front of the range, which was still hot.

"Please."

He leaned against the marble counter, thinking that at any moment she would pop giggling out of a closet. On the far side of the iron sinks was an arched wooden door, painted white. A long brass bolt had been thrown across the frame. Standish pulled back the bolt and opened the door. He stepped outside into the middle of the arched trellis.

"Hello!" he shouted. Then he realized that the door had been bolted from the inside.

He went back into the kitchen. Once more he walked all around the kitchen, hearing nothing but the sound of his own footsteps on the stone floor. His emotions swung wildly free within him, vacillating between frustration, rage, disappointment, amusement, and fear without settling on any one of them. He put his hands on his hips. "Okay," he said. "We'll play it your way." At length he went back up the narrow staircase. On the table in the suffocatingly formal dining room were his folders, the cover over his food, the bottle of wine.

Dinner could wait another few minutes. He went back into the pantry, opened the liquor cabinet, and removed the bottle of malt whiskey and two glasses. The bottle said COMMEMORA-TIVE HERITAGE 70 YEARS OLD. He set the glasses down beside the sink and poured an inch and a half of whiskey into each glass, then replaced the bottle and carried the glasses into the dining room.

He sat down and drank while staring at the pantry door. The whiskey tasted like some smooth dark meat.

He finished the whiskey in his glass, picked up the other glass, and tilted all the liquid in it into his mouth and swallowed.

As he ate, he flipped through drafts of unfamiliar poems. They seemed to make even less sense than was usually the case in Isobel's poetry. Most of them seemed to consist entirely of randomly selected words: *Grub bed picture dog, Hump humph laze sod.* He wondered if Isobel had evolved toward or away from outright meaninglessness. He drank some red wine, which he noticed tasted as good as the Esswood whiskey, though in an entirely different way. Perhaps Isobel had written drunk. He revolved the bottle and looked at the label. It was a Pomerol, Chateau Petrus, 1972. And the veal was so good that it was almost worth eating at every meal.

In fact—

Standish stopped chewing for a moment.

In fact, it was like being with Isobel, eating this particular meal at this particular table. It was as if time did not exist in the conventional linear sense at all and she were somewhere just out of sight.

The P of the title meant *Past,* Standish realized.

He closed the folder of poems, pushed it aside, and drew the thick folder of the memoir nearer to his plate. He drank wine, he chewed at his food and drank again. He read.

An unmarried young woman from Duxbury, Massachusetts, came to a great estate in England. A beautiful woman named E. greeted her. E. led her up the staircase to a long gallery and a suite of rooms that overlooked a playing fountain. The young woman from Massachusetts bathed and rested before going downstairs to meet the other guests, knowing that she was in this place to find her truest self. She experimentally opened a door in her bedroom and discovered a staircase that seemed like a secret known only to her—

Standish tried to pour wine into his glass and found that the bottle was empty. A few mushrooms lay in congealed gray sauce on his plate. The brightness of the dining room hurt his eyes. Back in time again, he yawned and stretched. Somehow it had gotten to be nearly midnight. Standish stood up and went back to the pantry to pour himself another inch of seventy-year-old whiskey. If his body was tired, his mind was not—he would have trouble sleeping.

Carrying his folders and glass, he moved through the room to the main entrance, not feeling like struggling up his and Isobel's "secret" corridor this late at night.

He mounted the great staircase and took the right wing toward the little anteroom before the Inner Gallery. He knew that the door to the gallery was opposite the door to the staircase. Therefore he felt as if his body had betrayed his mind when he bumped into a large piece of furniture, somehow got turned around in the dark, and could not find the other door.

He told himself to stay calm. He ceased blundering from one piece of furniture to another. The room seemed even darker than it had when his beloved had led him through it. He forced himself to breathe steadily and slowly. In the darkness he could see the large clumsy shapes of high-backed leather chairs. All four walls seemed covered with a uniformly mottled gray-brown skin that refused to resolve into rows of books. He stepped forward and banged his right leg painfully against a hard surface. He swore under his breath, stepped sideways, and inched forward.

A space opened up before him, and he moved more confidently toward the hovering plane of the wall. After a single step he tripped over some low piece of furniture, screamed, and fell. The glass flew out of his hand and shattered far off to his left. He landed on his left arm, still clutching Isobel's papers. Sharp, definite pain shot from his elbow to his shoulder, then settled into a constant throb. Standish began to push himself along the floor like a grub. He realized that he was very drunk.

From somewhere above him, he heard a woman laugh.

His entire body grew cold, and his testicles shrank back up into his body. He tried to speak but his throat would not work. The laughter expired in a short happy sigh. The severed tendons of Standish's throat reattached themselves. "Where are you?" he whispered.

Silence.

"Why are you doing this to me?"

He heard a soft flurry of movement behind him, then thought he heard rapid footsteps moving down the staircase.

Standish groped his way across the room until his outstretched fingers found a wooden door.

He came out into the blaze of light that was the Inner Gallery, rubbing his eyes with his left hand. Reality wavered around him, golden plates and golden forks and a deserted mansion and severed heads and a woman who vanished into laughter and a baby not his baby in a past that—

The Birth of the Past.

He shook his head. He needed sleep. Cool drafts moved around Standish's ankles. He looked through the dark windows and saw the windows of the Seneschals' suite shining back at him.

While he watched, a small dark shadow scuttled across the shade of the window on the left, and the lights went off as abruptly as the slamming of a door. It had not seemed the shadow of an ordinary human being. All the contradictory feelings within Standish melted into a single act of acceptance: he was in the Land, and he would follow where he was led.

Standish let himself into the Fountain Rooms, moved unseeing through the living room, and threw himself onto the bed.

nine

... B orn in Huckstall, the fleeing blue-eyed boy it was?

Standish's bed stood beside the long pond in cool moon-light, and a disembodied voice had just spoken lines about Huckstall and a blue-eyed boy which, though nonsense, had caused a turmoil in his breast. The dark pond stretched out before him. He held a sleeping baby in his arms, and the baby slept so rosily because it had just nursed at his breasts, which were womanly, large and smooth-skinned, with prominent brown nipples. A drop of sweet milk hung from his left nipple, and with his free hand Standish brushed it away. The peace of holding the baby in the bed beneath the moon was a kind of ecstasy. Then he remembered the speaking voice and the creature in the window, and looked down the side of the pond to the group of leaning trees. Their twisting branches concealed a being, male or female, who wished to remain hidden. Standish felt a simple profound apprehension that this being wanted to harm his baby. It—he or she—would kill him too, but the threat to himself was a weightless scrap, a nothing against his determination to protect his baby. As if in response to the threat, his breasts tingled and ached and began to express tear-shaped drops of white milk that leaked, rhythmically as drips from a faucet, from his nipples.

From somewhere either in the depths of the silvery trees or beyond them a woman began to laugh—

—and in the darkness of the Fountain Rooms, without breasts or baby, Standish flew into sudden wakefulness. His heart banged, and his body felt as if it had been torn from an embrace. Someone else was in the room: the dream-danger had been supplanted by this real danger. Whoever was in the room had just ceased to move, and now stood frozen in the darkness, looking down at him.

The publican of The Duelists had told the truth and Robert Wall had lied: an American had been lured here and lulled to sleep with rich food and strong wine, and the murderer had crept into his room and killed him.

Standish felt with a horrible certainty that the murdered American had been decapitated.

He tried to see into the darkness. His baby had been taken from him, and a being who meant him nothing but ill stood wrapped in darkness ten feet away.

"I know you're there," Standish said, and instantly knew she was not.

There were no giggles now. Standish lifted his head, and nothing else in the room moved. He was now as alone as when he followed the woman's laughter down the kitchen stairs. Yet it seemed to him a second later that someone *had* been in the room with him, someone who circled all about him, someone who was a part of Esswood, Miss Seneschal or his beloved (it occurred to Standish that his beloved might actually *be* Miss Seneschal), someone who needed only the right time to appear before him. She could not show herself to him now, for he did not know enough now.

She would show herself when he had earned the right to see her.

He remembered dreaming of having large breasts so engorged with milk they leaked, and absently rubbed his hands over his actual chest, slightly flabby and covered with a crust of coarse black hair. Something about Huckstall pushed at his consciousness urgently enough to make him sit up in bed—he felt pricked by a pin. But what could Huckstall have to do with his work, which of course was the meaning of the baby in his dream?

Standish got out of bed to pee. A haze of light touched the bedroom window, and he turned just in time to look through the slats of the shutter and see the Seneschals' light snap off again.

ten

An impossible thing happened the next morning. On the way to the dining room by way of "his" staircase and corridor, Standish lost his way inside Esswood and found himself wandering around strange corners, down unfamiliar steps, past locked and unlocked doors.

Standish had suffered very few hangovers, but each of them had made him unreasonably hungry—he wanted only to get downstairs and devour whatever was on the table, even if it had a funny name and looked like earwax. He almost ran down the stairs. His head pounded, and his eyes were oddly blurry—no more alcohol, not ever, he promised himself. He passed through the remnant of the huge spiderweb and pawed at it in revulsion. After a time, it seemed to him that he had circled around and around so many times that he must have gone past the first floor. He slowed down. The walls of the staircase were of whitewashed stone that was cold to the touch. When had the walls changed to stone? He looked over his shoulder. The curve of the wall, the iron sconce, even the dim gray light seemed strange.

Soon he reached the bottom of the staircase. The corridor seemed both like and unlike the one he knew. Just ahead was a tall door and a dim hallway. Everything seemed a little darker and dirtier than he remembered. He could not be certain that he was in a new part of the house until he had hurried down to the end of the corridor and found a blank wall where a statue of a boy should have been. He turned the corner and saw another, smaller flight of steps leading down to a concrete floor.

He stopped moving. Now it seemed to him that he had turned both right and left, blindly, several times without paying attention—his stomach had led him. He had a vague impression, like an image from a dream, of corridors branching off in an endless series of stone floors and dingy concrete walls. He felt a flutter of nausea. He turned around. A dark hallway extended past thick wooden doors and ended at a T juncture. He groaned. For a moment the sense of being lost overwhelmed his hunger. He backtracked down the hallway and tried the nearest door. It was locked.

The next door opened into a room filled with irregular thin white things, bits of kindling. Dusty frames containing dead moths and butterflies hung on the wall. High in the opposite wall was a little window like a window in a prison cell. The air smelled dead. Standish peered into the room and recognized that the objects piled on the floor were bones. Dozens, perhaps hundreds, of skeletons had been dismembered here. He suddenly remembered the story of Bluebeard's wife, and the ache in his head instantly became a red-hot wire of pain. Standish looked up and down the corridor and took a step into the awful room.

Skulls with long antlers lay in a corner. Standish walked nearer to the piles of bones. Many of them looked like the bones of animals. The faded colors of butterflies in a frame caught his eye, and he noticed a handwritten label taped beneath the glass. Nile Expedition, 1886. He began breathing again. Some cracked old Seneschal who fancied himself a naturalist had brought back these bones and butterflies from Africa in a crate.

He left the roomful of bones and hovered in the corridor. He could not retrace his steps through the series of rights and lefts he had unthinkingly taken. Opposite the bone room were two more doors, and Standish stepped up to one of them and opened it.

Things he could not see moved out of sight—he had an impression of fat little bodies diving behind the stacks of newspapers and magazines that filled the room. He imagined that malevolent eyes peeked at him, and thought he could smell fear and hatred. His eye snagged on the headline of a *Yorkshire Post* that lay on the floor, as if one of the little creatures had dropped it. PREGNANT WIFE, LOVER TORTURED THEN BEHEADED. *Grisly Discovery on Huckstall Slag Heap.* From somewhere quite near came a sly, breathless *tick tick tick* of sound that might have been laughter.

Standish stepped back. The entire room seemed poised to strike at him. He backed across the threshold and slammed the door. Standish felt light-headed, scared, unexpectedly brave— his discovery of this part of Esswood could not be accidental. He had been intended to find his way here. There were no accidents, no coincidences. He was *supposed* to be here. He had been *chosen*.

He tried the other door on that side of the corridor, and found it locked. Standish moved to the end of the corridor and went slowly down the steps.

A lower, narrower hallway led to an open door to a tiny cement room in which a greasy armchair two feet high sat beneath a hanging light bulb. On the far side of the chair was another door. Standish stepped inside. To one of the cell's concrete walls had been taped a reproduction of a painting in the Fountain Rooms—a small dog scampered before a carriage drawing up to Esswood. Standish crossed the room and opened the other door. Beyond it was a dark chamber that contained a huge squat body with a Shiva-like forest of arms that snaked to every part of the low ceiling. Gauges and dials decorated the furnace, and beyond it other machines leaned against the far wall: penny-farthing bicycles, a row of axes in descending sizes like a hanged family, a sewing machine with a treadle, a vacuum cleaner with a long limp neck and a distended bladder.

This was the library's rhyme, Standish saw. Up there, subtle spiritual things breathed and slept in file boxes; here, dirty things pumped out heat.

He went deeper into the basement. Standish peered into rooms filled with dolls and broken toys, with five cribs and five baby beds and five black perambulators as high off the ground as a princess's carriage, with musty folded sheets and blankets, with faded children's books, wooden blocks, and stuffed animals. He came to an ascending staircase and looked back to see the flaring nostril of a rocking horse through an open door. He had found "Rebuke's" *rooms of broken babies and their toys.*

The unfamiliar stairs took him up past row after row of wine bottles in tall cases like bookshelves, then transformed themselves into a wide handsome set of stairs with an onyx balustrade that led him into the splendor of the East Hall.

Breakfast had been laid on a fresh white tablecloth. Standish sat down and lifted the golden cover. The smoked corpse of a fish regarded him with dead eyes. Standish slid onto his fork a pasty mess that looked as hairy as a caterpillar. He put the paste in his mouth and bit down on a pincushion. Small sharp bones stung every square millimeter of his palate. Other slender bones slid between his teeth. He spat onto the golden plate.

eleven

S oon after, under the eyes of the great-great-great-great-grandfather and the pointing god, he nudged the bones lodged between his teeth with his tongue and made notes to himself on a legal pad. *If truly no accident or coincidence in universe, then narrative is superseded for everything is simultaneous. To be here is to be within Isobel's poetry, literally and metaphorically, for world without coincidence is world which is all metaphor. It is childhood once again. Key to the nonsense poems. Syntax the only source of meaning.*

Question: toys dolls beds, etc. seen by Isobel, as in "Rebuke." What happened to the children that used them? Why "broken"? How many children did Edith Seneschal have?

Must ask Seneschals about siblings.
Could the secret be some horrible family disease?
Standish thought a moment, then wrote another line.
Research in churchyard?

He looked down at the pad for a moment, then ripped off the sheet and wrote a few words on the next. This too he tore off, and took it outside the library door and laid it on the carpet. When he returned to the desk he looked at his guardian spirits and decided that he had spent enough time on the poems for the morning. *B.P.* was what he wanted to read.

With a happy sigh he pushed the poems aside and pulled the bulkier prose manuscript toward him. He began reading on page 26, where he had broken off the previous night. For some twenty minutes Isobel's handwriting squirmed before him on the page. Then time ceased to be a linear sequence of events, and Standish entered the Land with Isobel.

The young woman from Massachusetts found herself growing fonder of the house each day. A happy accident had led to her meeting her hostess, E., the well-known patroness of the arts, in Boston; and when E. had asked to see the young woman's work—and been impressed by what she described as its "bravery"—she had invited her new friend to join her at her estate. So the young woman felt an initial gratitude to E., but the speed with which she worked, once introduced to the Land, warmed this emotion to love. She found herself writing both prose and poetry more easily than ever before in her life, coming into her own voice a little more surely every day. And after readings in the West Gallery during the evenings, she was praised and applauded by writers whom she had earlier known only as revered names. Encouraged, she began to jettison from her work nearly everything that made it resemble the poetry of her own time.

That's my girl, Standish thought.

The young woman from Massachusetts spent her mornings writing in the Fountain Rooms, took lunch with E. and the other guests, and in the afternoon wandered through the Land—her name for Esswood. The physical world excited her nearly to euphoria. She felt that Esswood's beauty called to her, spoke to her, welcomed her. In the afternoon guests not busy writing played croquet, bathed in the pond, read by themselves in the library or the East Hall, or read to one another beneath sun umbrellas on the great terrace overlooking the pond and the far fields. Dinners were lavish: gourmet meals and great wines. The young woman declared a preference for loin of veal with morel sauce, and did not object when the Land teasingly offered it to her every night for a week. The wines too were ambrosial. On her first night the guests were given a 1900 Chateau Lafite-Rothschild, and on the second night, an 1872 Chateau Lafite-Rothschild. On the third night the guests were given an 1862 Lafite-Rothschild, reputedly the greatest vintage of the past hundred years, and considered likely to surpass all other wines for the next hundred as well.

The young woman's euphoria was more substantial than that given by wine, more permanent than could be provided by good company, and more profound even than that found in artistic progress. The feelings the young woman began to associate with the Land were not overtly religious, but were intensely spiritual—a force like music or disembodied spirit seemed to inhabit every aspect of the estate. What was most remarkable about the web of feelings linked to the Land was its release of gaiety. Not naturally high-spirited, the young woman joined the other guests in play—charades and tableaux and laughing conversations.

The young woman found herself indulging a previously unsuspected taste for practical jokes: she used her "secret" corridor to move unseen about the house, and delighted in disarranging a fellow poet's papers or effects, and in appearing like a specter in their rooms at night, then vanishing.

Riveted to the pages before him, Standish felt his heart slam against his ribs.

Although she had never taken any great interest in children, the young woman felt that much of the Land's strange and tender appeal to her was due to her hostess's two surviving children.

Again, Standish's heart nearly stopped.

E.'s calm was all the more remarkable in the light of her children's fates. She had married a second cousin with the same surname, a man uninterested in either the arts or country life and far more devoted to French brandy, Italian women, and the House of Commons than to his family: yet he had given her five children, three of whom had died in their earliest years. The two living children, R. and M., endeared themselves to the Land's young guest by their quiet, sweet, rather stricken charm: they had little energy, for they too were supposed to have contracted the disease that had killed their siblings. This awful disease, it was rumored, had been transmitted to the children by their father, and was something of a family curse; a family secret, too, for the exact nature of the disease was not known.

Both children tired easily, and were often inordinately hungry—it was a symptom of the disease that to sustain even low levels of energy, the sufferer had to take in large quantities of food, though what sort of food remained a mystery. The children were always fed in private. Despite their special diet, little R. and little M. seemed to be wasting away before the young guest's eyes. The sister more so than her brother: while *he* could still appear to be something like a normal child, *she* was weaker by the day. *He* was pale; *she* was pallid, even waxen. At times the poor child's skin seemed damp and oddly ridged, or pocked, or swollen, or all three at once, and so white as to be almost translucent—as if she were in the process of changing into another kind of creature altogether.

Standish looked up and saw that the light in the library had grown rich and golden. His watch said that it was one-thirty. He was half an hour late for lunch. Numbly, he got to his feet.

He knew that he had not even begun to assimilate what he had read. He would have to understand what Isobel had written even more than Isobel had understood it. This seemed crucial: Standish had heard the music too, and he had experienced Isobel's euphoria the first time he had stepped out into the Land in daylight. But Isobel had taken everything at face value. The words *timeless, eternity, gaiety, children, disease, transformation* swirled through Standish's head. *Specter, laughter, disembodied spirit.*

An idea of the morning presented itself to him with even greater force, and he walked on complaining legs to the great door. When he opened it he saw an ignition key on the carpet.

After lunch, groggy from veal and wine, he opened Esswood's great front door and inhaled fragrant summer air. For an instant he pictured the two living children, little R. and little M., seated on the marble steps. Then he saw the car on the drive and gasped. It was a Ford Escort, painted turquoise.

Standish flew down the steps, noticing that the car was far cleaner than the one he had driven from Gatwick to Lincolnshire. He was sure that it was a different car. When he reached the drive he walked up to it and touched its warm, smooth, well-waxed hood. It *was* a different car. Like everything else that had been taken into the Land, it shone and sparkled.

Standish got in behind the wheel and fit the key into the ignition.

It took nearly an hour to find the local church. When Standish finally forced himself to stop and ask for directions, he found that he could scarcely penetrate the harsh, slow-moving local accent. Trying to make sense of the garble of lefts and rights given him by two grudging men outside a pub, Standish wound up on Beaswick's High Street, where teenagers stared at his car and mumbled remarks he did not have to understand to know were obscene. The town was gray and dirty. Overweight women with piled-up hair and flaming faces peered into the car. Then, as suddenly as slag heaps and flares had turned into thick forest, the ugly little sweetshops and tobacconists' became open fields and desolate marshes.

Eventually he saw a six-foot heap of grass and earth bristling with thick roots at an intersection and remembered that one of the hostile men before the pub had told him to turn one way or the other at a "hummock." Perhaps this was a hummock. Far away stood a farmhouse. Two swaybacked horses stared gloomily at him from the middle distance. On the other side of the hummock a hill led up to a small gray church and a graveyard of tilting headstones. On the crest of the hill above the church stood a beehive-shaped windmill he had seen before. He was three minutes from Esswood: he could have walked across the field to get to the church.

Standish drove up onto the wet grass before the stone church and left the car to walk around to the graveyard.

On the other side of the church was a smaller, even uglier stone building like a cell with curtained windows. Standish walked between the two buildings to the cemetery gate.

Enclosed by a waist-high iron fence, the cemetery covered an acre of sloping ground and contained several hundred graves. The oldest headstones, those directly before Standish, resembled wrinkled old faces, sunken and blurred beneath a pattern of shadows and scratches. Standish began to move down the middle of the graveyard. None of the stones bore the name Seneschal. Other names recurred again and again—Totsworth,

Beckley, Sedge, Cooper, Titterington. He kept moving slowly through the cemetery.

A door slammed behind him, and someone began working toward him through the graves. Standish turned around to see a black-haired man in a long, buttoned cassock approaching with one hand upraised, as if to stop traffic. The vicar's heavy red face sagged as if against a strong wind, and he leaned forward, ducking his head, as he hurried toward Standish.

"I say, I say."

Standish waited for the man to reach him.

Close up, the vicar presented a hearty smiling manner that seemed a disguise for some other, more bullying quality. He was in his late fifties. The odors of beer and tobacco enveloped Standish as the man came nearer. He spoke in the harsh accent of the village. "Saw you from the vicarage, you know. Don't get many strangers here, don't get accustomed to strangers' faces." A big yellow smile in the red face, as if to balance what might otherwise have been simple rudeness. "American, are you? Your clothes."

Standish nodded.

"Interested in our Norman church? You'd be welcome to a walk round inside, but it makes me a bit uncomfortable to see a man I don't know walking about our little, um, our little garden of souls here. Seems irregular."

"Why?"

The vicar blinked, then showed Standish his false smile. "You might think our ways are odd, but we are just a tiny little bit of a community, you know. Just paused on your way through, did you?"

"No." The vicar irritated Standish so profoundly that he could scarcely bring himself to talk to the man.

"Came all this way to do grave rubbings. We've nothing to interest you in that line, sir."

Standish frowned at the vicar. "I wanted to see if I could locate any family graves. My name is Sedge, and my people came from this village."

"Ah. Well, now. You're a Sedge then, are you?" The vicar was squinting at him, half-smiling, as if trying to make out a family resemblance. "Where did you say you were from in America?"

"Massachusetts," Standish said. "Duxbury, Massachusetts."

"You should find Sedges right the way through this little cemetery. When did your people arrive in America, then?"

"Around eighteen fifty, maybe a bit earlier," Standish said. "I traced us back right here to Beaswick, and a local family invited me to stay with them, so I wanted to see if I could find any of their people here too. I'm curious about them."

He turned away from the vicar and began inspecting headstones again. Capt. Thomas Hopewell, 1870–1898. An angel leaned weeping back from an open book. A marble woman shrank back from grief or death, her face over her hands—he recognized the statue as the twin of one at Esswood. Behind him he felt, with senses suddenly magnified, the exasperation of the vicar. He waited for the man to come thundering after him, and then realized that the vicar's manner was that of a man with a secret.

The soft heavy tread came up behind him. "Local family, is it? Might I ask which local family?"

"Of course." Standish stopped moving and turned around to the sagging red face. Behind the vicar he caught a glimpse of a marble monument atop a child's grave—a small boy reaching up with outstretched arms. This too was a copy of a statue in Esswood's "secret" corridor. "The Seneschals."

The vicar actually licked his lips. His entire manner had changed in a moment, along with the atmosphere between himself and Standish. "That's really very interesting, that is."

"Good." Standish turned away to inspect the name on the base of the monument of the grieving woman. SODDEN. He fought the impulse to giggle. "Where are they buried, then?"

"Prominent family, of course." The vicar scuttled up beside him. "You'd say, *the* prominent family in our little corner of the world. You're putting up with them, are you, Mr. Sedge? In Esswood House?"

"That's right."

"Quiet over there, is it, Mr. Sedge?"

"Yes, it's very peaceful," Standish said.

"I daresay." The man licked his lips again. Standish was startled by the sudden realization that the vicar looked frightened.

"I think it's strange that I don't see any of their graves. Edith's children, I mean—the three who died so young."

"Strange? I should think it is strange. And what about Edith herself? Miss Edith Seneschal, who became Mrs. Edith Seneschal, now surely you would think she would be buried here as well. Wouldn't you, Mr. Sedge?"

The man was peering at him with his head cocked and his lips pursed. Rusty brown stains like stripes covered his cassock.

"And her husband too, don't you think? The Honorable Arthur Seneschal, a dim figure granted, a willing partner one might say, very willing I'd wager, in all his wife's ambitions, you'll be wanting to see his headstone as well, won't you?" There was a venomous lilt in his voice, and Standish had the feeling of some unspoken complicity between them.

"What's wrong with you?" he said.

"He wonders what's wrong with me," the vicar said to the air. "Mr. Sedge is curious, isn't he? The odd fact is, there hasn't been a Sedge in Beaswick since seventeen—what was it now?" He darted over the low grass to a tilting headstone. "Seventeen eighty-nine, I thought it was that. Charles Sedge. A bachelor, by the way. An only son. He'd be amused by your story. He'd be especially amused that you claim to be staying with the Seneschals." The vicar astonished Standish by leaning over the tombstone and braying: "This fellow claims to be a Sedge—long-lost American cousin, Charles! Wants to pay his respects. Says he's putting up at Esswood House. Wants to find the graves of Edith's children. Can you give him any assistance, Charles?"

He straightened up. An unhealthy mirth had turned his face an ever darker shade of red. "Or perhaps I heard the name wrong? Did you want to say that your name is Titterington? Or Cooper? You couldn't be a Beaswick Sedge, in any case, could you? They were all dead by the time you claim your family arrived in America. And no descendant of a Beaswick Sedge would walk through the doors of Esswood House."

Standish said, "I don't know what you're talking about. Are you accusing me of lying?"

"I'm accusing you of ignorance," the vicar said. "I wonder where you really are staying. I wonder where you really are from. If you don't know that we would refuse to give burial to any Seneschal, you have no connection to Beaswick. Which makes me wonder what it is that you are doing in my churchyard, telling me tales about staying at Esswood House."

"Why shouldn't I be staying at Esswood House? I am staying there—I'm a guest, I was invited—"

"Nobody is staying at Esswood House. I very much doubt whether anyone is still living in Esswood House. There are a couple of students hired to discourage intruders and keep the place clean, but they're not local people—not even Lincolnshire folk." He looked down at a flat grassy grave and rustled the folds of his cassock. To Standish it looked as though the vicar were dancing inside his body, whirling about in furious glee. "You needn't think I'm so stupid I can't see, that I'm such a blockhead I didn't know what you were immediately I saw the cut of your jacket." A joyful defiance filled his eyes. "I knew someone like you would appear—someone from a tawdry American magazine, some bit of trash you'd call a newspaper—but it never in my most ambitious dreams came to me that when a jackal like you appeared you would claim to be looking for the graves of Edith's children."

"But that's what I *am* looking for!" Standish shouted.

Now the vicar was virtually twitching. "Then you'll need directions to Esswood House, won't you? I saw how you came up—I saw your car. You didn't come from the house. You drove from the village."

Standish thought of protesting that he had lost his way. Instead he said, "What's the quickest way to get to the manor?"

"Aha! Truth! The unfamiliar guest, truth, has entered our conversation. To reach Esswood House you proceed straight back the way you came until you reach the hummock, then turn right, not left, and proceed directly on past the Robert Wall—"

"The what?"

"The Robert Wall—it's only a local name, needn't be alarmed. I thought the gutter press would be less easily startled. Won't fall down on you, the old wall's been standing on the boundary of the Seneschal estate for four centuries."

"Why is it called the Robert Wall?"

"Because, I suppose, a man named Robert built it. He wanted to keep the Seneschals in, didn't he?"

Standish began walking away. He brushed past the vicar without looking at him. The vicar stepped back on a grave and laughed. "You're going to discover their secret, is that what you're going to do, Mr. Sedge?" Standish heard him laughing as he walked past the ugly church.

twelve

Two days later, at the end of the afternoon, a sentence at the top of the page jarred him back into the waking world.

I have found my vagrant, my scholar-gipsy with corn-flower eyes.

It was a surprise to see Isobel stoop to the conventional period mush of "cornflower eyes," but the young woman from Massachusetts had found a soul mate, someone with whom she could take long walks and discuss literature. *I have found my vagrant*—Standish remembered the mad creature who had materialized on the outskirts of Huckstall, shuddered, and continued reading. Isobel found the vagrant an untutored genius, a lone figure in the world, without wife or child. At the bottom of the page Isobel had written *Matter for another tale.* The "vagrant" promptly disappeared from the manuscript.

Standish read for the rest of the day. The library faded away around him and he wandered through the Land with Isobel. The details of her days did not vary much, but Standish found the similarities to his own routine very pleasing. In Isobel's descriptions of writing, eating, strolling around the house and its grounds, an unstated purpose, some transformation, hovered just out of sight. Whatever the young woman looked at burned in her vision. The long pond *simmered,* the far field was *a green hide nailed to the sun.* The library was an *oven, a volcano,* and poetry was *lava.* Every surface *shimmered* and *gleamed,* everything *trembled* with the pressure of the force beneath it.

Until nearly eight o'clock Standish remained immersed in Isobel's memoir, not so much reading as *being read.* His boyhood and the other, more real world that existed within or beside this one took shape around him, and with it came the memory of Popham, the feelings and atmosphere of the wonderful and terrible time that had really begun when in his Burberry on a blazing day he had tracked Jean to another's apartment and really ended with the nurse who was not a nurse and the bloodied sheets around a discarded utterance, a non-noun, an aborted word in a deleted sentence. There was a truer self within him, and he had felt it struggling to be born.

A superstitious vicar in a stained cassock could not hope to understand it.

When he looked up and noticed that it was nearly dinnertime, Standish was aware of a tremendous glory, like the beating of a great pair of wings, in the air around him. For a moment, the library seemed charged with an absence, not an abrupt withdrawal, but the anticipatory, trembling absence just before the appearance of a radiant and necessary being.

This time Standish took the longer route to the dining room. He moved almost ceremoniously to his chair and lifted the cover from the veal in its sauce. Beside the gold-rimmed glass on the tablecloth was a bottle, streaky with dust, of Chateau Lafite-Rothschild, 1862.

After dinner he took the main staircase to the upper floor. The sound of absent laughter filled the air of the little study; so did the odor of malt whiskey, from both the glass he had spilled two nights before and the one he carried before him, aiming it like a key at the study's opposite door. He emerged into the Inner Gallery. He thought he heard a small agile body skittering out of sight behind him—dodging back into the shadows. No, the vicar of Beaswick would not, would never, understand. A folder of papers nestled between his elbow and his ribs.

He was not drunk. He was not. He was moving in a straight line down the gallery between the big panes of glass and the looming paintings, and he could have touched his nose with his finger. On his right side English horses grazed in a painted field; on his left, the Seneschals' windows glowed pale yellow, and in their bedrooms two Seneschals, male and female created he them, lay separate or entwined in their beds or bed. Standish heard sounds from the courtyard, and stepped nearer the windows and looked down. A glittering shower of diamonds, lava, golden blood, shot upward and flew apart before falling back to earth. This eruption resolved itself into a fountain illuminated by lights sunk into the gravel around its base.

Esswood was taking him in, accepting him, *using* him, as it had used and accepted Isobel.

He placed the folder on the bed, undressed, and went into the bathroom. A flushed, radiant demon filled with blood gazed at him from the mirror. Standish brushed his teeth, his eyes held by the gleaming eyes of the demon in the mirror. Froth bubbled comically from his lips. He rinsed his mouth with cold water, spat into the sink, looked once again at his demon's eyes, then splashed his face with cold water.

His cock stuck out before him in the mirror, rigid as a ruler and curved slightly upward. A translucent drop appeared at its tip.

Standish masturbated over the pretty blue-patterned sink, as he did so fantasizing that he stood in the grove of twisted, gestural trees in cool night air. A certain woman stood by the edge of the long pond, outlined by the silver moonlight so that her naked body was a curved pane of pure black. He could feel crushed leaves, small twisted roots, and rounded stones beneath his feet. Cool air prickled the skin on his arms. The hieratic figure by the pond stepped forward. Her eyes shone white in the blackness. Standish gasped, for he actually *was* out in the cool night beside the pond, not in the bathroom of the Fountain Rooms. What he felt—the chill, the leaves beneath his feet—was what he felt, not a fantasy, and the beloved woman, who with her shining eyes and outlined body seemed half a tiger, moved forward again. His body uttered a massive affirmation, a million nerves slammed one door shut and threw another open, and gouts of semen shot out of him like the water from the fountain and flew into the darkness. Standish instantly felt drained, as if he had lost a quart of blood. The terrifying figure before him seemed to be smiling in acceptance of his offering. He closed his eyes in terror and fell down in a faint—

—but opened them in the bathroom, where he had propped himself against the sink with locked arms. A final cloud of white semen oozed across the pattern of blue flowers. The gooseflesh was fading from his arms. He shook his head and looked at himself in the mirror. His face was tired and ordinary, white with shock. He splashed his face and swished water around in the sink. He felt as if he had just stepped out of a roller coaster.

In the bedroom, he buttoned himself into clean pressed pajamas which had been laid out on the bed. His cock felt hollowed out. When he got into bed he first smelled, then saw, the glass of malt whiskey he had placed on the bedside table. Unhesitatingly he picked up the glass and swallowed half the contents. A ball of warmth began to grow like a seed in his stomach. Now he felt light, nearly boneless. The folder fell from his hands onto his chest. Just before he fell asleep he realized that he had not looked to see if the Seneschals had turned off their lights.

But they had turned them off when he awakened several hours later. Once again he had the feeling that someone was in his room, but this time the alien presence was not frightening. His bedroom was utterly dark, without even the faint haze of yellow on the louvers of the shutters. From the presence in the room flowed a sense of unhappiness, even of rage, too powerful not to be felt.

That she had returned at all spoke of how much she needed him.

"I know you're here," he said softly.

And then William Standish nearly fainted, for a slight form paler than the rest of the room separated itself from the darkness and advanced a minute distance toward his bed. Until that moment Standish had inhabited a world of suppositions, hypotheses, imaginings, and fancies—but the figure shyly advancing toward the bed was a proof, a confirmation. His mouth went dry.

The pale figure drew nearer. Now he saw that she was holding something before her with both arms. It was a baby. His heart moved with sorrow. He could see the top of the figure's head, and her hair falling in long smooth wings. Her paleness gave her an insubstantiality like transparency. She looked faded, worn away, like cloth that had been rubbed against a stone. Above its wrapping he could see only a portion of the child's face, a waxen nose and lifeless eyes. The woman slowly began to lift her head as she continued coming toward him. He saw her wide forehead, her thick eyebrows, the bridge of her nose—his emotions jammed together like a traffic accident. Taller, thinner, plainer, more intense than his beloved, this was the woman whom he had seen looking up at him from beside the long pond. Later she had appeared in the library window, looking down at him. She was Isobel Standish. Isobel was awkward and willful, sensitive in all the wrong ways. He realized that he more or less disliked her on sight.

She needed his help.

As if this were all that she had come to tell him, Isobel Standish turned away and began to melt back into the darkness with her baby. "Don't go," he said, and groped for the switch on the bedside light. Sudden stabbing light froze everything in the room into place, as if the candlesticks and the heavy press and the blue sofa had come to life in the dark and now had to pretend to be inanimate again. The woman with the dead baby had vanished. Standish heard water splashing in the courtyard and a loud rasping sound that was his own breathing. He began to shake.

There was no point in trying to get back to sleep. Standish threw back his covers and got out of bed. He rushed to the window and peered through the slats of the shutters. The Seneschals' windows flashed like a signal and went dark again.

He could still feel the cool air on his bare skin, the prickly roughness of the leaves beneath his feet, and how the being had called him, how it had smiled and hungered. . . . White dots appeared before his eyes. He sat down. Then he lifted his left foot and saw that the sole was black with dirt. Small dark particles clung to his skin. His blood actually seemed to stop moving. He lowered his foot. Here and there on the carpet were dusty footprints the size of his feet.

For a moment Standish knew beyond doubt that flabby white creatures moved all around him in the dark house, searching for his traces, needing him: he could hear the grown sick babies crawling in the secret corridors and the Inner Gallery.

Once chosen . . .

Standish jumped up and turned on another light. He picked up the folder. *Birth of the Past,* he thought—that was an Esswood title. He sprawled on the blue sofa to read until morning.

thirteen

I sobel's handwriting had degenerated into a nearly illegible scribble. Entire paragraphs tied themselves up into private code that insisted on staying private. Lying on the blue couch, almost too frightened to read, too frightened not to read, Standish recognized the signs of great emotional pressure.

The young woman from Massachusetts, now no longer quite so young, had returned to the Land. In the three years of what she thought of as her "exile," her work and her marriage had deteriorated. She had written nothing worthwhile since leaving Esswood, and had ceased to tolerate the attentions of her husband. She felt that her appearance had deteriorated, leaving her with limp hair, dull eyes, and a sunken face. It was as if she had been cut off from some necessary nourishment. In great pain she had written to her "savior," "the gardener of her soul," and begged to be invited back. *Of course,* E. had written, *we have been waiting for you.* The husband had apparently decided not to oppose her going, and indeed must have known by his wife's raptures that to try to keep her from going would be to end his marriage. Martin Standish, as astonishingly complaisant as ever: perhaps he had thought to save his wife's sanity by giving her Esswood once again. After seven weeks' travel, the young woman collapsed into E.'s arms at the train station and soon was driven up the gravel drive between the trees. A small brown-and-white King Charles spaniel yapped at the wheels of her carriage. She wept the instant she saw the Palladian facade. She was home again. *We have needed you,* E. said to her. That night, she ate loin of veal with morel sauce and felt health and strength returning to her body. In honor of her homecoming, E. said, they drank an 1860 Chateau Lafite-Rothschild. The life she had needed, the one that gave life back to her, had again taken her into its arms.

Standish looked up and saw moonless night through the chinks in the shutters. A faint murmurous sound that had faded in and out of his awareness revealed itself to be the splashing of the fountain. He guessed that it was something like four o'clock.

For a time the young woman was conscious of nothing but her joy in being reunited with territory so sacred to her. She took her chair in the library in a daze of happiness. She wandered down the terraces and crossed the fields, letting them soak into her. She often found herself weeping, as if her life had been rescued from a barely perceived danger. The pitch of perception she had reached three years ago now returned effortlessly, and everything about her carried the charge of its own energy. The earth *burned*. The bindings in the library *gleamed*, the fat white sheep *blazed* in the fields. Poetry came in a vivid, almost frightening rush that left her exhausted and trembling. Every day there were two, three, four new poems— and dozens of pages of her journal. She was like an adept of a religion that worshipped creation itself, for what infused the Land with energy and made her writing leap sizzling onto the page was an original sacred force without a god, without Jesus, without priests or ceremonies—a transfiguring force that was its own god, savior, priest, ceremony. She had been *chosen* more decisively than before. She would never leave by choice, and if someone dragged her away—if she were expelled like waste into the inert world of Brunton Road, Duxbury, Massachusetts— she would inhale gray death and die.

For among the other guests was the "vagrant," the "scholar-gipsy" who had helped awaken her. The famous cornflower eyes seemed dimmed and faded, his clothing even shabbier, he was not perhaps even notably clean—to Standish he seemed a distressingly seedy character. Yet they worked side by side in the library, they dined together, they walked together in the summery fields. They spent many hours in the Seneschals' suite with E., who had fallen ill, and her son. The girl's illness had progressed, and she was kept secluded in another room. *My daughter cannot be seen,* E. said, waving away their request with a limp hand. *She is on a journey she must make alone—though she has needed you, my dear. We have all needed you.* The boy, as beautiful as ever, like his sister with the same hawklike beauty of their mother, had become abstracted and wan. He slept most of the day, but when awake he seized the young woman's hand and begged her for stories. *We have all needed you.* The young woman caught on both their drawn grave "hawk" features a look of hunger that was more a cast of features than a passing mood, as if it underlay all their charm and accomplishment.

Stung out of his trance, Standish looked up. A faint light had begun to seep through the shutters. Outside the house, hundreds, maybe thousands of birds seemed to be spinning in circles, raising an amazing joyous clamor as they flew round and round.

Need and hunger, thought the appalled Standish. Hawk features.

Did he know of the secret staircase and the secret corridor, the young woman asked her scholar-gipsy. She saw in the raised eyebrow that he thought she was teasing him—adding a literary mystery to their tale. I'm not joking, she said, there really is a secret staircase. Oh, is there now, asked the scholar-gipsy. And what have you been reading, you Duxbury romancer, *The Castle of Otranto*? *The Monk*? No, nor *Varney the Vampire*, she answered, but how do you imagine I travel about the house without being seen? Do I transport myself by magick? Show me, my girl, I am in your thrall, uttered the scholar-gipsy, and the young woman led him up the grand staircase and through the disused chamber that in the days, now gone, when E.'s husband had deigned to spend the Parliamentary recess in Lincolnshire had been his study, which was a misnomer for any activity ever carried on in *that* little room— and when were the servants ever going to do anything about that wonky light (as E. called it)?—and then down the Inner Gallery past the view of the fountain, not neglecting to wave to the dear grave boy watching who knew what from his mother's window, and into the young woman's cherished Fountain Rooms. Her soul mate admired the stuffed fox and the terrarium while she slipped into the other room and through the door to the staircase and called out, *Can you find me?* He homed toward the sound of her laughter. And opened the door and came through to join her behind the walls, saying Cowslip bluet lily hyacinth rose. Now you know my secret, she said. And took him down the long staircase to the library. *I hear strange creatures moving here at night. But I have an advantage, strange night-creatures or no.* No—you have *the* advantage, said the vagrant scholar-gipsy, you have a special place in this house, you have been taken in, you heard E., they need you. Because I need them more, she said, and he smiled and shook his head. Yet sometimes I feel quite terrified, a great change is coming upon us all and I do not know if I have courage for it. Then, because he looked puzzled and downcast, she said, *Behold, I have mysterious treasures*, and took his hand in her private realm behind the walls and led him down and down the staircase until they were in darkness beneath the earth. You will see what I have seen, she said, and led him through a rat's run of stone passages.

You can find your way back?

Oh there is no way back but to go forward.

At length she gripped his hand and said: *Here.* It was a passage like any other, stone and dark and lined with doors. She threw open the nearest and said, Here is the chamber of the bones, where previous guests have gathered. Who is laughing? he said, following into a vault heaped with dry nibbled bones, not you nor I, but some laughter follows us. The treasure is laughing, said she, and took him out and down and through another door where three great doll's houses stood side by side beneath a reproduction of the painting in which a gay King Charles spaniel scampers by the right offside wheel of a carriage coming up to Esswood House. The doll's houses reproduced Esswood House in miniature, and in one front window of each little house a low light as of a candle burned.

Inch-Me and Pinch-Me and Beckon-Me-Hither are landlords here, she said. Within each house are rooms with little golden plates and little golden goblets and the room where little wine bottles fill rack upon rack and the dark little library where Inch-Me and Pinch-Me and Beckon-Me-Hither pretend to read like the great grand folks upstairs. And I must still show you the enormous furnace room where the live furnace they tend burns and burns, and the last room, the final room, the as you might say ultimate room—and they both heard a stir of sound behind them and turned, the young woman with an almost fearful ecstasy to see not whatever it was that she expected, but E.'s young son, the inheritor of the Land and all its treasures should the miniature live furnace continue to burn in his narrow live chest, Robert.

Of course, said William Standish to himself, and heard that the birds had ceased their racket. I knew it all along. I knew who he was. And I knew who *she* was, too.

Looking for poems? the boy asked. I often wondered where poems come from, and now I see two poets and I know. Have you seen enough of our cellars? I can show you other aspects, if you please? His smile played, and the young woman and her scholar-gipsy pleased that he show them wonders, new wonders. And the boy took them past the furnace room and the tiny chair empty of the tiny furnace-tender and up into the house again and through the screened passage and outside into the blazing warmth. The boy's face, so like his mother's, was full of an odd translucent light thrown up by the marble steps. He led them through the trellis to the top of the terraces.

E. and several other guests sat upon a Turkish carpet unrolled in the shade, and their hostess waved to the party of three. The other guests were G., a poet newly arrived in London from Yorkshire, N., a painter of portraits, and his mistress, O., so pale and weary of attitude that the young woman suspected her of indulging in opium, Y., D., and T., young novelists who had come down from Oxford to vanquish the literary world, lived together in a house in Chalk Farm, and reviewed books for *TLS,* and J., a literary banker and book collector from New York. These were not a particularly brilliant bunch, the young woman felt. Even E. had lost interest in Y., D., and T., whose labored epigrams, languid mannerisms, and excessive enthusiasm for the wine cellar had assured that they would never receive a second invitation.

All of these people waved to the threesome that crossed their vision, and E. called out to the young woman as she might to a servant a request that she speak to the cook about the quality of the lamb to be found in the local market—the young woman had come to be involved in some of the day-to-day matters of the house.

They clattered down the iron staircase to the long pond and the gnarled trees. The boy Robert led them to the trees, saying, Oh, in all your wanderings did you ever wander *here*? I hear the laughter again, the vagrant said, who is laughing? He thought to balk, but the young woman took his hand and pulled him after the dancing boy into the trees. Inch-Me and Pinch-Me and Beckon-Me-Hither, said she. The gamekeeper's boy, said the vagrant, looking out for foxes. And does old William have a boy now, called out Robert, I thought he lived without woman or get. Our young lady must be right, though I doubt I ever heard the names ere now.

From the terraces it looked as though only a small number of trees separated the pond from the fields, but in fact a considerable growth of trees lay beyond the pond, the illusion created by a valley or fold in the land into which the boy led them now. Sunlight fell in patches and spangles on the soft ground. My brothers and sisters are here, you know, he said, and the ground became level again and the trees separated before him like ladies drawing back from an unpleasantness. A round clearing lay open to the sun but out of sight of the house, visible only to the kites and blackbirds overhead.

Three low mounds occupied the center of the clearing, which was overgrown with long, silky grass. The young woman's first thought raised gooseflesh on her arms: the long extremely comfortable-looking grass appeared well fertilized, well *fed* that is: and she tightened her grip on her friend's arm. They have no headstones, he said, and answered the boy, They need none, we know their names. His young face filled with sly shadows. A magickal place, the young woman thought, thinking magick by no means as comfortable as the long-haired grass. A bird, some bird, cackled in the midst of the trees. You see our heart, I suppose you might make poems of it, the boy said, and his face became so complex the young woman cried aloud—from pain or fear she did not know.

The boy was gone when she looked up from the protection of the scholar-gipsy's arms, and a dizzying male scent seemed to raise her from the ground. She was weeping in the pouring sunlight, and the gipsy kissed her and she moaned and the gipsy lifted her and lay her on the grass and made her clothing and his clothing disappear as he kissed her neck and shoulders; and she screamed with joy as he thrust his torch within her and they made love not for the first time and not for second or third, nor even the tenth or the twentieth.

Standish put down the pages. His outside, his shell, seemed to have detached itself from his interior and be capable of movement while the interior Standish, the real Standish, sat numb and frozen. He was visited by the acute memory of standing sweating in his hat and raincoat on the Popham street and looking up at the window behind which his loathsome treacherous friend was screwing his equally loathsome and treacherous wife. He should have expected exactly this, he realized: Isobel's return to England was too passionate not to be at least partly romantic, of course she had been having an affair all along. Martin Standish and Duxbury, Massachusetts, had stifled her talent, and the "gipsy" who had set it free had killed her by fathering her child.

"They flee from me," Standish said to himself—

—and saw again, as from beneath the brim of a hat on a hot airless night as traffic hummed and roared like bees at his back, a lighted window in an apartment building. The bee-noise shook the world. A week before Jean had told him that she was pregnant, and expected him to believe that the child was his.

Standish shuddered, and for a moment feared that he was going to vomit upon the manuscript. *B. of P. Birth of the Past* or *Birth of the Poet? Betrayal of the Professor. Bastard of the Pretender.*

Childish giggling laughter came to him from the next room. He pushed the manuscript aside and watched his body get out of bed and cross to the door and open it. His body must have wanted to do this, because the inner Standish could not command the body to stop. All was well, however, all was well. The scampering little people from the basement had not overturned any tables or broken any lamps. He began to relax. Then both inner and outer Standish froze again. On the rug before the door to the Inner Gallery lay a long white envelope.

He *had* heard them. Inch-Me and Pinch-Me and Beckon-Me-Hither had come and left a message. Welcome to reality, it would say, you don't need your hat and raincoat now, no more standing about on street corners with a dry mouth and a pounding heart. No, sir! He stepped up and looked fearfully down at the envelope. It bore an English stamp, his name, the Esswood address. His name and the address had been written in a sloping, pushed-together handwriting he gradually recognized as his wife's. Standish bent down and picked up the envelope. It had been postmarked in London.

He experienced a wave of instantaneous and pure revulsion. Jean and the magpie in her belly had tracked him down: they could not give him even a week's seclusion. They would crowd through the door and waddle in, dripping cookie crumbs and shreds of doughnuts.

Braced for everything, braced multidimensionally, Standish sat down, ripped open the envelope, and removed his wife's letter.

fourteen

Dear William,

I bet you didn't expect to hear from me so soon. It's the funniest thing, yesterday I ran into Saul Dickman, who said that he was spending the rest of the summer in England. He only wished he was going to be in a cushy spot like you, with an exciting project like yours. Anyhow, I asked him if he could take a letter with him and mail it when he got to London, and if you get this, that's what he did. Three-day delivery, not bad, right?

I wanted to write for a lot of reasons—William, you seemed so tense before you left. When I took you to the airport, you were frothing at the mouth whenever anyone passed us, and when they called your flight you were so worked up you wouldn't have said good-bye if I hadn't reminded you. You had that awful look in your eye. This makes me so worried. But I don't know how much I should say, because I don't know how mad you'll get. Anyhow, I sure hope you got some sleep on the plane because some of this was just plain old lack of sleep. And William, you were never really a relaxed kind of guy anyhow, were you? I mean, a lot of stuff is just kind of normal for you, and I guess I'm not perfect either, you know what I mean.

But you know why I'm worried, too. You should know. I don't want to make you mad at me, and things have been pretty good between us for the past couple of years. But neither one of us will ever forget what happened at Popham. Of course everything was hushed up and you landed on your feet. I got over it. We managed to forgive each other, didn't we? You even got another job. But it still happened. William, I don't ever want any of that to ever happen again. I'm not going to lose this baby, you can bank on that, but it's just as important that you take care of yourself.

If you start feeling that old way again, just come home. COME HOME. Don't lose yourself. Don't forget me. Everything is all right.

Zenith is nice, but couldn't we live anywhere? As long as you stay William.

I need reassurance too. A lot of it, like you. I don't know if I'm trying to give it to you or to me by writing to you like this—I know I'd find it really hard to say *things like this to you in person. I hope you'll write to me or even call me, maybe just to cheer me up. I'm so heavy I can hardly walk to the bathroom, and I pee every time I burp. I have heartburn that won't go away. I'm afraid that something is going to go wrong—I know there's no reason for this, but I'm afraid that it'll be like that other time, our terrible time, and that I'll have to talk to lawyers and policemen, and when I get so worried I wish you were here so I could see you were okay.*

Please write, do good work, and come home soon.
Love,
Jean

P.S. I looked up your place in a reference book, Oxford Companion to English Literature*? Something like that. What a place! Have you found out ANYTHING? Is there really a big dark secret? Or shouldn't I ask?*

fifteen

Saul Dickman, Standish thought. That figured. Yesterday I
ran into Saul Dickman. Yesterday I just happened to find
myself talking to good old Saul, who's been married twice and
can be counted on to see the sex object in even an abject blob
of hysteria like Jean Standish. Standish crumpled the letter and
threw it into the wastebasket.

Showered and dressed, he emerged into the Inner Gallery
twenty minutes later. A small razor nick beside his Adam's
apple printed a constellation of red-brown spots onto his
collar as he walked past the windows. He twisted his neck to
look at the Seneschals' windows, and imagined seeing a boy

with a shadowy angelic face, the younger duplicate of Robert Wall's, staring back at him. He could not see the boy unless he looked with Isobel's eyes—and then he could see, with dreamlike clarity, the dark-haired boy who would grow up to call himself Robert Wall, leaning against the glass across the way. The boy followed him in a manner that looked casual at first but was actually charged with an electric attention. It was what *they* had seen as they walked through the Inner Gallery. The seeming languor, the actual hunger. *It's better never to leave Esswood*—that was how they did things, by tossing these gauzy little spiderwebs over you and seeing if you figured out the pattern before they melted away. Oh, you were ten years old in 1914, were you, Mr. Robert Wall? And are you implying that your general appearance at the age of eighty-six, not to mention your sister's at the relatively even more astonishing age of eighty-three or four, is part of the reason why it's better never to leave Esswood?

Standish passed into the dark study and saw in his mind the eyes of the woman who had come into his room with her dead baby: he imagined Isobel locking him in her arms, clamping him into her stony embrace, all that desperation pouring itself into a romantic mold and overflowing it.

He ran down the staircase, seeing everything as it had been seventy-odd years earlier. These old men were two generations nearer, and what went on beneath their gaze was a deliberate mockery. Earlier Seneschals had lived quietly, buried their dead, improved the library, and hidden their afflicted. Unfortunates like the late Mr. Sedge had fed their awful appetites. Through Isobel's eyes Standish saw the riot with which Edith had replaced the secretive old order. Imaginary throngs sprawled over the furniture, talked ceaselessly, raided the wine cellar, stripped the kitchen of its food. They dirtied the sheets and stained the carpets and filled every room with a blur of sound and smoke and color. Chattering, impudent ghosts—full of spurious accidental "life," some of them diseased, some of them coughing into their fists, some of them as drunk as Jeremy Starger, some as prissy as Chester Ridgeley, some men always pawing at women's breasts, touching touching, some women glancing always at men's fly buttons, in secret touching, like Jean Standish on the other side of an upstairs window in Popham. In the East Hall he saw them standing in pairs, twisting their hands together, their lips moving in their endless clever talk-talk, never dreaming what dreamed about *them* from behind the walls and waited.

You have been chosen, said "Robert Wall."

He gasped in the sudden heat as he trotted down the stairs. His clothing felt hot and confining, and he yanked the blazer off his shoulders and tossed it aside as he reached the bottom step. Standish ran over the gravel to the side of the house and ducked into the trellis.

A hot swarming smell, sharply sexual, surrounded him. From behind the interwoven green walls and ceiling came a steady intense live buzz of sound, as from a hive. Standish burst out of the trellis, expecting to see a swarm of bees or wasps dancing over the terrace, but the air was clear and hot and empty. The intense, sizzling noise continued, coming from everywhere at once. Popham: the sweat dripping down his forehead. Standish paused and wiped his face on his sleeve. Imaginary guests looked up from their lawn chairs and tilted beards and sharp eyes at him and pretended to flick dust from the sleeves of their perhaps too carefully selected garments. He turned from their whispers as Isobel had done and trotted toward the iron staircase. Large dark splotches rose up out of his body and printed themselves on his shirt. Beneath the thin distracted heat-sounds emanating from real insects and the faint susurrus of leaves from the grove beyond the pond, there endured the buzzing of a hive, as of busy indifferent traffic at the back of a man in a Burberry raincoat in Popham, Ohio, on a night as hot as this. A week before she said she was pregnant. And expected him to believe the magpie was his. He reached the staircase and ran down the terraces in the sun.

At the bottom he could see with Isobel's eyes the slight figure of a beautiful boy, in a cream shirt perhaps, open at the neck perhaps, watching with tilted head from the top of the rusting staircase. No gamekeeper's boy, for old William lived without woman or get. Standish pretended to be indifferent to the traffic on the Popham street outside the apartment of a man whose name he would never permit even now to enter his mind except in disguise as when the eye fell upon the wrapper of a CERTAIN cough drop or in suchlike contact, as if you loathed a gentleman named Park and on a business trip to Gotham found yourself in Central.

Try not to think of a white bear. Standish had grown very good at not thinking of white bears.

The buzzing humming hivelike noise of the Popham street became louder at the bottom of the terraces.

Standish began moving more slowly toward the grove of gestural trees at the right of the long pond. It was from here that the hivelike sound came, and as he passed between the first of the trees Standish imagined that this sound underlay the earth everywhere, that it was an impersonal world sound, not to be noticed anymore, like the word Park unless you were in Central.

The twisting trees were oaks, hundreds of years old. Long ago they had been deformed by some process equivalent to foot-binding. The limbs rolled out and splayed into labyrinths around their thick dwarfish bodies. His ferocious beloved had stood here, watching him.

Standish gazed through the branches to the green rise of the fields, dotted with fat unmoving sheep.

Nothing is known once only, nothing is known the first time. A thing must be told over and over to be really told.

Before him, invisible except as a fold in the landscape from even the topmost terrace, the trees continued down a slope and gathered so thickly that he could not see the bottom of the slope. He began to move downhill. Eighty years ago when these trees were young, there would have been paths through them; now the branches had grown together. Standish had come down ten or twelve feet, but the locked trees would not allow him to go farther. He circled sideways, searching for an entrance to the web, and finally he moved back a bit toward the pond and got to his knees and crawled beneath the locked branches.

sixteen

Beneath his hands was a smooth brown carpet of crumbling leaves and loose pebbly earth that felt as if it had passed through the digestive system of an enormous insect. The dwarf oaks formed a kind of low arched entrance, though Standish saw none of the patches of light through which Isobel had moved on her way to the clearing. The darkness increased as he worked his way forward, and he found himself moving wearily through an intermittent night. After a time Standish knew he was lost. He had inadvertently crawled away from the path to the clearing. His knees were wet, and his hands were gritty. Standish collapsed onto the damp earth. Sweat steamed from his body. He lay his head on the backs of his hands. The earth hummed and moved in almost impalpable tremors like the shifting of an animal's hide. He forced himself back to his knees.

Perhaps five minutes later the darkness modulated into mild gray, and soon after that sunlight began to pierce the locked arms of the trees. Blotches of light struck the ground. His back heated. The hive noise had grown louder, more dense, many voices working together to form one great voice. Then Standish was where Isobel and the gipsy had followed the boy Robert, for the interlaced fingers had separated above him and he was looking down at his squat square headless shadow.

The sizzling noise had ceased—he was at its center. Standish grunted himself up onto his feet. His knees were filthy and soaked, and his shirt was dark with sweat. He stood on the far edge of a circle of trees surrounding a round clearing perhaps fifteen feet in diameter, like something stamped out of the woods by a giant machine. Long soft grass blanketed the clearing. At its center stood the three mounds Isobel had seen. They were barely distinguishable from one another and the ground beside them. They have no headstones, they need none, we know their names.

Standish exhaled, understanding everything at last, and heard the sound instantly disappear into the louder but still inaudible sound of the soul-traffic that was the noise of the hive. *Magick*, Isobel had written, using the old spelling, and for once she had been right. It was magick. It had always been a sacred place, probably, for that was one way to put it, but now it was more so because of the people they had used and buried here. Edith was not buried here, and neither were any of her children, for none of them was dead. Others were.

Standish went through the grass and stood before the mounds. With a groan he threw himself down onto the mass grave. Against his cheek the grass felt like the long cool hair of his beloved. He spread his arms and embraced the grave. The sun poured down on his back. He groaned again, and gripped the silken grass with his fingers. Down in the soil with Isobel lay a lost child who screamed for release with all the others, screaming like a pale creature pressed against a window.

What power a lost child has, what a lever it is, what a battery of what voltage.

Standish pushed himself off the grave. He made a feeble effort to brush the dirt and broken leaves from his trousers. Then he wiped his dirty hands on the sides of his trousers and gazed up at the birds wheeling overhead. They had the proud wingspread of predators, raptors. Esswood's center kept shifting, widening out as one thing rhymed with another in the poem it was. Standish turned from the grave toward the circling wall of trees. Directly before him was the path on which Isobel and her lover had followed young Robert Seneschal to the clearing. In the earth beneath the twined branches he could see the marks of his own passing. He lowered himself to his knees, which cried out in pain, and began to crawl back into the woods.

In what seemed half the time of the trip to the clearing, light began to reach him and the trees separated and he was looking at the slope leading back to the pond and the first terrace. He stood and walked up the slope, now and then grasping a branch to pull himself forward.

seventeen

At the top of the iron staircase he walked across the burning grass toward the trellis. A crowd of languid ghosts raised their teacups and from the corners of their eyes watched him pass. Standish slipped into the trellis. Fat green leaves, dark as spinach, cupped the trembling liquid of the sunlight. He entered the house through the unbolted kitchen door and moved toward the stairs to the pantry and dining room. Beside these enclosed stairs was a door he had not tried earlier. It opened onto the basement stairs.

Downstairs, he turned toward the furnace room, retracing backward his earlier route through the basement. Doors stood open in the stone passageway, and he passed the room filled with stuffed tigers and dusty plush dogs. All the doors he had opened remained open. Standish hurried along.

He turned through the open door of the concrete cell with its small worn chair. In the picture on the wall the playful dog scampered at the carriage wheel. Standish went through the second open door and proceeded past the black furnace to the far wall to the family of axes.

He took the largest axe from its bracket, hefted it, replaced it in the bracket, and took the next largest. This one felt less likely to tip him over. He carried the axe back into the corridor.

From the furnace room he trotted up the short flight of steps toward the two locked doors he had tried on his earlier trip to Esswood's basement.

At the top of the steps he came out into another dark corridor. Here were four closed doors. Standish walked toward the first, swinging the axe beside him as he went. This was the second locked door he had tried, beside the room stacked with old newspapers. He twisted the knob. The door was still locked. Standish stepped backward, lifted the axe over his head, and swung it at the middle of the door.

The head of the axe sank into the wood. Standish yanked it out and swung again. Sweat blinded him. He rubbed his eyes with a dirty hand and smashed the axe into the door again. Finally the door began to splinter, and after several more swings Standish was able to put his arm through a hole in the wood and turn the knob from the inside. A knife of raw wood cut into his arm, and blood bubbled happily from the wound and ran down his arm.

Standish opened the door.

He had expected big dollhouses, cut away on one side to allow a child access to every room, but these were actually

miniature Esswoods, larger than he had expected and identical to their model down to the water stains dripping from
the corners of the windows. They were actual houses, doll
bungalows, lined up like houses on a suburban street. High
on the wall above, like the sun in a suburban sky, hung
another reproduction of the painting in his sitting room—
the capering dog, the rolling carriage. A low light burned in
each third window from the right. Standish's breath caught in
his chest. It was as if three little people were due home from
work any minute now. The floor was a mess of small white
bones—chicken bones—so dry they snapped when Standish
stepped on them.

The stairs before the miniature houses were of marble,
cut by craftsmen who had been extravagantly paid for their
silence. He looked into one of the windows and saw tapestries
two feet long and carpets three feet square, and ornate red and
gold chairs a foot high. There would be golden plates three
inches across, and golden forks half the size of his little finger,
and little wineglasses that would snap in his hands. And did
they sleep on beds, or had Edith ordered them pallets woven
from soft wool? And had they screamed at night in pain and
terror, and had Edith come down to comfort them?

That was not very likely, Standish thought. Their mother
had been like God in the heaven of the picture above their
houses, loved or hated but invisible—vanished into the sky.

Before Edith's generation, had there been other Seneschals
who occupied the little houses, afflicted Seneschals who lived
concealed from everyone who came to the great house around
them? That was likely, for in the twentieth century the only
man Edith had found to marry had been her unsatisfactory

second cousin, who likewise had found no one but Edith to marry *him*.

And had any of Edith's illustrious guests ever known or suspected her secret? That was even more likely, Standish thought, for after a time all who came were scribblers like Y., D., and T., and eventually no one at all came: no cars, no carriages for little dogs to follow. And think of what they had written! Henry James and his mad governess who arrived at a remote house to care for two afflicted children, E. M. Forster and his tale of people living in a great hive, Eliot's wasteland and hollow men . . . Many of Esswood's guests had walked part of the way into knowledge. Isobel had gone farther than any of them, and Isobel had never left.

It's better never to leave Esswood, Standish remembered.

He stepped back, raised the axe, and brought it down on the first little house. The thin plaster wall crumbled like stale bread, and little paintings in little frames and little chairs and a little bed fell from a guest bedroom into the West Hall. Another blow smashed the main staircase into splinters and toothpicks. Another shot miniature books from miniature shelves, and cleaved the portrait above the mantel. The floors broke apart like kindling, and the foot-high furnace fell into clanking sections of pipe. The library's vaulted ceiling shattered into a rain of candy. Standish swung his axe again, and the contents of a kitchen cabinet exploded upward into the ruins of the dining room. A table three feet long slid down a tilting floor and crashed into a miniature sink. Matchstick bones and tissue butterflies flew up like tinder. The East Hall disintegrated, and the bedrooms of the East Wing splattered against the wall. It took Standish nearly an hour to smash the first little house into a heap of broken shreds and shards from which protruded a length of bookcase, a porcelain sink, a little book bound in Moroccan calf, and the curved wooden corner of a window frame. Then he moved on to the second house, and a little more than forty-five minutes later, to the third.

When that one was destroyed too he threw his shirt behind him. His arms felt as if he had been rowing through heavy seas, and his back was one vast ache. Standish dropped the axe, and it smashed a patterned china teacup to powder. He picked up the axe again and discovered from a sharp stab of toothache in his right palm that he had developed a blister the size of an orange. He settled the axe handle into the blister and felt the sharp awakening presence of pain.

The other locked door stood across the cement corridor. Standish spared both the axe and his hand and kicked at the stile beside the lock. The door rattled in its jamb. He kicked again with the flat of his foot, then drove the whole strength of his leg against the lock. It broke with a loud snap like the breaking of a bone, and the door flew open on its hinges. Standish dragged the axe into Isobel's ultimate room.

There was no window: the light came in with him. He wiped sweat from his forehead and waited for his eyes to adjust. A dry *tock tock tock* that sounded faintly like frightened laughter came to him from the corridor.

At last Standish could see that he had broken into an empty room. He was not sure what he had expected—nothing as overt as skeletons or a chopping block, but something that would *shake* him. The floor sloped toward a central drain. Before the back wall the cement floor was scuffed, as if a heavy piece of equipment had stood there a long time. There were long faint scratches in the floor. Finally Standish saw what appeared to be a series of oblong frames on the wall to his left. They reminded him of the framed butterflies in the bone room, and as he stepped nearer he saw that the frames contained photographs.

There were six of them, ordinary snapshots of unremarkable couples. From what Standish could see of the clothing worn by the two people in the first photograph, it had been taken in the late twenties or early thirties. In the third photograph, the man wore the uniform of an American army officer. Thereafter the men reverted to suits. The women next to the first two men wore veils; all the other women wore large-brimmed hats, or had turned their faces from the camera, or were in shadow. Two of the photographs had been taken on the first terrace of Esswood House, and two had been taken on the path that circled the long pond—shadows of the twisted oaks turned the woman's face to darkness. Then Standish recognized the face of one of the men beside the pond.

The face was sunken and unhealthy, with prominent knobs of bone above the eye sockets, and the man's shoulders had a decided stoop. He was smiling—smiling in ecstasy. It was Chester Ridgeley, some ten or eleven years older than when Mr. and Mrs. Standish, William and Jean, had left the serpent-infested Eden of Popham College in the town of Popham.

But there was no Mrs. Chester Ridgeley.

The woman beside the old scholar had turned away from the camera into the shade of a deformed oak. She appeared to be in her mid-thirties, strong of body, square-shouldered, with the sort of inherent self-sustaining physical confidence with which even otherwise ordinary women are sometimes blessed, and which makes them anything but ordinary. Ridgeley held her hand trapped between his two old hands.

It was her because it had to be her. It was her because it could be no one else.

Standish went down the row of photographs and peered at each couple. The men, he guessed, were all academics— Esswood Fellows. The woman was always the same woman, always with the same air of physical confidence in the set of her shoulders, the carriage of her arms, the balance of her hips. In the fifty or sixty years represented by the photographs, she had not aged ten. When she had opened the door of Esswood House to him, she had appeared a strikingly youthful forty.

Standish stepped away from the photographs, aware for a moment that he was half-naked, dirty, out of breath, bleeding from many small cuts and abrasions, that he stank. . . .

He turned from the photographs and stared down at the drain in the center of the floor. He wondered if Ridgeley had ever returned to Popham. Had they received a telegram announcing his retirement? A letter declaring his intention to devote the remainder of his life to research on the life of that absolutely inessential literary figure, Theodore Corn?

I feel certain that you will understand my excitement at having made many discoveries here, also my unwillingness to sacrifice my remaining years to classroom lecturing when so much (and so much, also, in the personal sense) remains to be done. . . .

Standish left Isobel's ultimate room. Little bodies scurried here and there in the room stacked with old newspapers. He leaned in, and all motion ceased. Standish looked down at the copy of the *Yorkshire Post* and its blaring headline, then low-ered himself onto his sore knees and flipped the newspaper over and stared at the photographs he knew would be there.

But these photographs, of a burly publican with a face like a thrown rock, a hard-faced woman with high bleached hair, and a weak-chinned lover, were of strangers. *Tock tock tock* went the mechanical mirthless laughter. He forced himself up on his feet and looked down again at the meaningless faces.

A puzzling gap in experience, a piece of experience missing from the universe—a loss for which the universe yearned, ached, grieved without awareness of its suffering—went with Standish as he wandered with his axe beneath Esswood. He came to a modest set of stairs going upward to an open arch, and carried his axe up into the known world.

He passed through the arch and found himself at the back of "his" staircase, in "his" secret corridor that had been Isobel's. He walked down the hall to the dining room and opened the door. The smell of his cooling lunch was faintly nauseating. He went to the table and pulled the open bottle of white wine from the bucket. Then he carried the dripping bottle down the corridor.

The library seemed larger, lighter, even more beautiful than on the night "Robert Wall" had first shown it to him. The long peach carpet glowed, and the alabaster pillars stood like sentinels before the ranks of books.

Standish swigged from the bottle, then looked at the label. Another 1935 Haut-Brion, ho hum. He swigged again, and winked at Great-great-great-great-grandfather. He set the bottle on the desk and carried the axe across the shimmering room into the first recess. Here were the broad file boxes stamped STANDISH and WOOLF and LAWRENCE, all the names which had been the lures for the men whose photographs hung in the ultimate room. He had been right, his first day in the library, when he had imagined "Robert Wall" drinking blood from these fat containers.

Standish raised his axe and smashed open the second of Isobel's file boxes. A tide of yellowing paper spilled from the ruptured box and splashed on the floor. Standish swung his axe again, and the blister on his hand screamed like a child. Papers fluttered around him like birds. He drove the axe into the third STANDISH box, and instead of disintegrating into a shower of handwritten pages, the box slid along the shelf until it slammed into a wooden upright. Standish wriggled the axe out of the cardboard, and the box spilled off the shelf, dumping small square photographs to the ground like confetti.

Grunting with surprise, Standish bent down and picked up a handful of the photographs. And here, in the first photograph, was the image of a tall, intense-looking woman in a pale dress and close-fitting hat standing on the path beside the long pond. Standish knew that the dress was green, though the seventy-year-old photograph was black and white; and he knew the woman's face, in the photograph no more than a blur, had the long chin and narrow nose he had already seen. Here was Isobel at the chair in the library, here she was reading a fat book in the West Hall, here Isobel stood beside a rotund openmouthed man whom Standish eventually recognized as Ford Madox Ford. Standish tossed the photographs aside and grabbed another handful from the smashed file box. Isobel posed uncomfortably beside an equally uncomfortable T. S. Eliot. Isobel with a sleek dark-haired man who might have been Eddie Marsh; Isobel in the far field, trying to look pastoral; Isobel holding a drinks tray—serving cocktails—and smiling ruefully. The poor mutt.

Standish struck the box with his axe once more, and photographs flew all around him. Then he took aim at JAMES, and cracked the first one like a nut with one blow of the axe. Wads of loose paper cascaded out, and he kicked them apart.

He drove the axe into the second box of James' papers, and into the third, and then drove it down into the papers themselves and cut a great wad of them in half. Monuments of unaging intellect, Standish thought, and drove the axe into WOOLF. Then into the next file box, and the next, and the next, until every one had been smashed open and its contents spilled on the floor. After that he dragged the axe across the library to the second recess and started with FORSTER and BROOKE—ugh, how did he get invited?—and came to CORN.

Standish grinned at the thought of Theodore Corn. He smashed open the box. A few sheafs of paper flew out— Theodore Corn would of course have sheafs of paper, preferably slender sheafs—along with another gout of small square photographs.

The photographs hit the already impressive drift of papers on the floor with the clatter of falling insects. Standish bent down to pick up a random handful, assuming he would see more photographs of lumpy literary people.

They were strikingly like the photographs of Isobel. *I should have let this idiot's box alone,* Standish said to himself, feeling a premonitory tingle. He turned over various small squares of paper that had been printed with the same scant margins, the same dingy range of tones from sepia to light gray, and the same landscapes and furniture of Isobel's pictures. Many of the faces too were also in Isobel's photographs—Ford breathing through his mouth, Eliot hunching and making a face like a cat. The principal figure in this set of images was in some ways Isobel's male counterpart. A tall skinny figure in wrinkled suits, wearing unbuttoned shirts with flyaway collars, sometimes in a sleeveless Fair Isle pullover too small for him, he looked at the camera with a long lopsided rural face seamed and pocked by childhood diseases, adolescent acne, and a long attachment to alcohol. His left front tooth and incisor were missing, and his hands, twice the size of Standish's own, had joints like bolts.

What had reminded Standish of Isobel was none of this, but the man's air of aggrieved disappointment—the sense of having been cheated lifted from the photograph like an odor. Coarser than Isobel, he was just as embittered. His sly drunken face proclaimed *I deserve more, I need more.* Standish detested him even before he realized who he had to be, and then recognized that he detested him because he recognized himself in the man. If this person were an American of the 1980s instead of an Englishman of seventy years before, he might be married to someone like Jean Standish and be teaching in some dead Midwestern Zenith. He would dress better and a crown would fill the gap in his mouth. He would profess the Nineteenth-century Novel, not very well but at least as well as William Standish.

Standish flipped over another of the dark little photographs and saw the man leaning against the back of Esswood House with a leer spread across his gappy mouth and a scarf tied around his neck like a rope.

He was, of course, Chester Ridgeley's darling, Theodore Corn.

Then Standish realized that he knew one more piece of the puzzle—Isobel had taken these photographs, just as Corn had taken all the photographs of Isobel.

And this led to the final fact, as Isobel might have said the ultimate fact, which had prompted Standish's sense of foreboding when he had seen photographs spilling from Corn's box. The ninny Corn was the man Isobel had met at Esswood. Theodore Corn was her vagrant, her scholar-gipsy. He had been the father of her lost child.

Standish held the loose wad of photographs in his hands for a moment entirely empty of thought or feeling. He let them drop, and they clattered onto the strewn papers. Standish kicked at the mess on the floor. Everything about him seemed meaningless and dead. The meaninglessness was worse than death, because the meaninglessness existed at the center of a mystery, like the whorls of a beautiful pink and ivory shell that wound deeper and deeper into the glowing interior until they came to—nothing.

Theodore Corn looked up at him from a hundred photographs, sly and hayseed and unknowable.

Standish waded through the ruck of papers and smashed the axe into POUND. Another mass of papers flew up from a shattered box and fell, thick as leaves, to the ground. He saw Isobel seated beside Theodore Corn at the dinner table, gazing at him over the golden rim of her wineglass. He swung his axe and demolished another box.

Eventually Standish waded out of the second recess and went to the desk. The original file still sat beside the red gilt chair. Atop the desk stood the bottle of Haut-Brion. Standish looked down at Isobel's poor papers and considered carrying them over the recess and tossing them on the pile. He nudged the papers with his foot and watched them spill sideways, exposing lines and sentences of Isobel's busy handwriting. That was good: that was better. Now the sentences could lift off the page and escape into the sky.

Standish put the bottle to his mouth and drank. He examined the library impartially and found it beautiful. He looked up, and the god glared down at him, pointed his ineffectual finger. The god was made entirely of paint a fraction of an inch thick, and that the finger came forward to point was an illusion created by a man named Robert Adam, who had loved great houses and fine libraries. Standish hefted the axe in his hands. He raised it and let it fall on the desk. The axe cracked its top open. Objects Standish had not noticed, Bic pens and legal pads, fell into the desk. Other insignificant things went sailing into the library.

Late afternoon sun came streaming through the windows.

Standish dropped the axe and saw blood spatter onto the carpet. The carpet instantly drank the blood, shrinking the red spots and hollowing them into pale pink rings almost invisible against the peach.

As hungry as the house, his stomach growled.

Standish thought for a moment, then smiled and sat at the ruined desk. He found a pen nestled beside long polished splinters. He wrote *matches* on a legal pad. Then he tore the sheet off the pad and wobbled toward the door.

In the dining room the table was set for dinner. An open bottle of red wine stood on the tablecloth. Standish's mouth felt as if he had been eating ashes, and he filled the gold-rimmed glass to the top and gulped several mouthfuls before he bothered to look at the label. 1916 La Tache. It could have been the year Isobel returned to the Land, in search of immortality and the greedy embraces of Theodore Corn. What else had Isobel been looking for in 1916, in the midst of a world-engulfing war? The final curve inside the pink shell, the story inside the story, the new sentence, the source of the sound. Standish's hand slowly dripped blood on the tablecloth, and the tablecloth sucked the drops to pale circles. He smiled, and set down the glass to wrap his right hand in one of Esswood's broad linen napkins. Then he sat and lifted the golden cover. Isobel's meal steamed on the golden plate.

Standish ate. The room tilted to his left, then to his right. His whole body ached. Eventually his eyelids insisted on coming down over his eyes, and he lowered his head to the table and slept. In the midst of a grove of trees a shining baby lifted its arms and tilted up its head for a kiss. Standish stretched out his torn arms, but his feet were caught in thick silken grass like ropes. Blood dripped from the palms of his hands, and the shining baby turned its face away and cried.

Standish too wept, and woke up with his wet face cradled in the bloody napkin wound around his hand. "Oh, God," he said, imagining that he had to go back to the library and write a book about Isobel. A tide of relief radiated out from the memory of what he had done in the library.

He wiped his face and stood up. The axe lay beside his chair like a sleeping pet, and he carefully knelt and reached for the handle. It glided into his hand and fitted itself into the folds of the napkin.

Standish dragged himself down Isobel's secret corridor to the library. He toiled through the great empty space and opened the main door. On the carpet of the West Hall lay a large yellow box of Swan kitchen matches.

Standish carried the matches back into the library, leaned the axe against a column, and went to the second recess. He pushed open the box, and an astonishing number of matches fell out into the heap of papers and photographs. He stared stupidly at the box for a moment before realizing that it was upside down. He turned it over and saw that the other, uncovered end of the box still contained hundreds of matches. Standish removed one and scratched the head against the crosshatched strip. The match exploded into bright flame.

He bent down and touched the flame to the corner of a piece of paper. As soon as the paper ignited, he moved the match to another sheet. Then he tossed the burning match far back into the recess. A thin wire of smoke ascended, and a curl of fire followed it.

Standish backed out of the recess and watched the flames eat at the papers. The paint on the bookshelves blackened and burst into circular blisters just before the fire jumped to take the wood beneath the paint. Then he crossed the library to set the papers in the other recess alight.

He dropped the rest of the matches on the floor and left by the main doors. He had more than enough time to do what had to be done next.

Standish went out into the entrance hall. An ornate clock on a marble table told him that it was five minutes to ten.

He wandered down the screened passage and tugged at the front door. Velvet darkness began at the edge of the light that spilled from the house. The trees beyond the drive were a solid wall reaching from the dark ground to the vivid purple of the sky. Overhead were more stars than Standish could ever remember seeing, millions it seemed, some bright and constant and others dim and flickering, in one vast unreadable pattern that extended far back into the vault of the sky, like a sentence in a foreign language, the new sentence that went on and on until first the letters and then whole words became too small to read.

Standish walked out to stand beneath the great sentence. All of that writing in the library, the pages stuffed with words like bodies stuffed with food, would float upward to join the ultimate Esswood that was the sentence in the sky. Beyond it, invisibly, did an angered god point a finger from a whirling cloud?

Standish carried his axe back into the house.

eighteen

As he went up the stairs he caught the faint odor of burning, but when he turned off to the left into unfamiliar territory the faraway smell of smoke faded into the odors of old leather and furniture polish and the fresh evening air that entered the house through open windows. He passed under an arch at the top of the left-hand wing of the staircase and went into a room that was the larger counterpart of the study on the other end of the house.

A light fixture hung from the central rosette. Empty bookshelves covered two of the walls. A single rocking chair had been pushed up against a bare wall with pale rectangles where pictures had hung.

At the far end of the empty room was another arch through which Standish could see a bleak corridor. A bare light bulb dangled from a cord. Dust gathered on the floorboards, and cracks ran across the plaster walls. Two large windows with brown shades stood on one side of the hallway, two dusty brown doors on the other.

These were the windows he had seen from the Inner Gallery and the Fountain Rooms. He tugged on the ring of a window shade and gently released it upward. Across the dark courtyard his old windows glowed yellow around the outline of a misshapen child-sized figure peering out. Standish froze. Inch-Me or Pinch-Me or Beckon-Me-Hither stared at him, and Standish stared back. Then the small featureless shape disappeared. A gray whorl of smoke moved into the frame of the window. Standish imagined the secret stairs filling with smoke dense enough to push back at you if you tried to move through it. Another, deeper rift of smoke appeared in his window.

He still had all the time he needed.

Standish turned from the window and placed his hand on the first doorknob. He quietly opened the door.

Light from the corridor spilled into the first few feet of a room in which Standish made out the shape of an iron bed, a cheap wooden chair, an open suitcase on the floor. Paperback books lay scattered around the chair. He moved through the opening and closed the door. In the darkness he became aware of the pain in his hands and his back. Oily grime covered his body. He could smell fear, sweat, blood—he stank like an animal in a cave.

Inside his head he heard the sound, more an echo than sound itself, of a baby crying. Standish began to move on tiptoe across the room toward the untidy bed. When he was a foot or two from it he was able to make out the pattern on the thrown-back coverlet. The sheets were white and rumpled, and the dented pillow lay across them like a fat slug. From the wrinkled sheets floated up an odor of perfume and powder. A spattering of his own blood fell on the sheets.

Standish turned around and left the room as quietly as he had come in. The door let yellow meaningless light flood over and around him.

In the window on the other side of the hallway he saw the reflection of a crouching half-human animal, its body smeared with dirt and blood, come creeping around a door. It carried an axe in one hand. With something like glee, Standish saw that this stooped, monstrous creature was himself—the inner Standish. Twenty-four hours ago he had glimpsed him in the bathroom mirror, but now he was really out in the open. It seemed that he had been waiting for this moment all of his adult life. *"Why, Miss Standish,"* he whispered, and pressed a hand to his mouth to keep from giggling.

Through the creature's body he saw the square of fire that was the window of his old room.

He turned toward the next door. The bent creature with the axe turned too. Bloody matted hair covered its shoulders. Its dark hand was still pressed to its mouth. He watched the creature float down the corridor until it moved out of the window.

A few mincing steps brought him to the second door. His slippery fingers touched the knob. He ground his teeth and soundlessly turned the doorknob. The door moved inward a few inches, and Standish tiptoed with it. A few inches more, and he slid into the room.

A pair of shoes stood on the bare floor. A white shirt draped over the back of a chair glided toward him like a spirit out of the breathing dark. He closed the door behind him. The shirt looked like a spirit waiting to be born, it may be through the pair that occupied the bed across the room. Slow sweet exhalations and inhalations came from them. Over his own stink Standish caught the delicate scent of perfume and the other, coarser odors of sweat and sex.

He sighed.

As his eyes grew used to the dark, he saw the bare dim walls that would be white in daylight, the masculine clutter of socks and sweatshirts and jeans on the floor. A tennis racquet leaned against the wall. The bed was an untidy tangle of long white limbs and wild hair.

Now Standish felt as if he had awakened from a long trance. He was simply himself, what all the days, weeks, hours had brought him to. He was a stunted monster carrying an axe. For perhaps the first time since his childhood, Standish entirely accepted himself.

"Mnnn," came a voice from the bed.

Standish stood inside the door breathing slow shallow breaths. He could imagine himself in bed with the couple, lying in a loose tangle of arms and legs, absorbed into them.

But soon they would begin to hear the fire and smell the smoke. He waited until they had settled down into one another's arms and begun to snore light, funny, almost charming snores. He stepped forward. There was no response from the bed. He took another gliding step forward. The beautiful double animal on the bed lay still. Standish moved directly beside it and raised his axe.

He swung it down with all his strength, being both the executioner out in the tundra with his chopping block and the bureaucrat at his desk. The axe landed at the base of one of the animal's two heads and almost instantly cleaved through the vapor of the flesh and the fishbones of the spinal column. The animal's other head lifted itself from the pillow just as Standish raised his axe again and presented a perfect target, extended in disbelief and confusion which ended with the axe's downstroke.

Now the bed was a bloody sea. Standish dropped the axe and plucked both heads off the soaking sheets by the hair and lowered them to the floor. He picked up two pillows, yanked them from their cases, and tossed them back on the bed. Without looking at either of the faces, he stuffed the heads into the empty pillowcases and carried them out into the hallway. They were surprisingly heavy, like bowling balls. Standish trotted down the hallway in misty smoke, went through the arch, and into the barren room at the top of the stairs. The heavy pillowcases swung at his sides.

Black smoke had accumulated against the ceiling in cloudy layers. From what seemed a great distance came the sound of rushing wind. Standish passed through the opposite arch and looked down the left wing of the staircase.

Several distinct layers of smoke hung from the ceiling and moved toward him with a massive gravity. A wall of heat met him at the top of the stairs and pushed him back like a giant hand. As yet there were no flames before him. He began to run down the stairs, and felt as if he had stepped into an oven. The hairs in his nose crisped painfully, and his eyebrows turned to smoke. He saw the thick hair on his chest, arms, and belly curl inward and turn to ash.

When he reached the main body of the staircase a combination of smoke and heat blinded him. He kept running with his right hand on the hot banister. The heads in their pillowcases rhythmically banged against the balusters. His skin felt scalded. His right hand struck the newel cap at the bottom of the stairs, and the things in the pillowcases slammed into the post.

Standish plunged through scalding black soup. A flat red glare exploded off to his left. When he reached the screened passage he sensed the thick tapestries writhing as their fibers shrank and dried. He ran straight into the door, bounced back, then grabbed the scalding knob with a hand wrapped in hot cotton cloth.

Frigid air rushed over him. Blind and coughing, Standish stumbled out onto the terrace. He tottered down three or four steps, then collapsed backward and wheezed, trying to fight the smoke out of his lungs. He landed hard on his bottom and lost his grip on the pillowcases. They slid out of his hand and bumped down the steps. Standish felt as if he had been blowtorched. Smoke poured from the fabric of his trousers and clung to his shoes. Down at the bottom of the steps, the pillowcases smoked like smudge pots. His legs took him down the steps, and he limped to one pillowcase, picked it up, then limped across the gravel and picked the other up too.

The heads tried to pull the ends of the pillowcases from his hands as he trudged over the gravel. After a few seconds he stopped to look back. Flames showed in the first- and second-floor windows, and smoke poured through the roof.

Standish carried his heavy trophies around the left side of the house. Something inside Esswood let go, and a thunderous crash sent a flurry of sparks and flames into the air. Standish trudged forward through a rain of fire and stepped over a burning chunk of Esswood. He was too tired to look back and see what happened.

Around the left side of the house and across the drive stood a long low structure with four sets of wide double doors inset with windows. Standish pulled himself toward the building and looked through the first window into an empty darkness.

Through the second window he saw an old saddle and harness hanging on the back wall.

In the third window reflected fire burst through Esswood's roof.

Standish looked through the fourth window and saw the back end of a turquoise Ford Escort. He pulled open the doors and carried the heavy pillowcases inside. As soon as he touched the car he remembered that he did not have the keys, which were probably inside the pocket of a pair of incinerating jeans on the second floor of the East Wing. He opened the door and collapsed into the driver's seat. The two sacks leaked onto the ground between his legs. He reached down and swung both the sacks and his legs into the car.

He put his hands on the wheel and stared at the dashboard, remembering movies in which people jump-started cars. Something heavy fell on the roof of the building. He smelled smoke, and his eyes filmed and his stomach churned. When he had finished coughing and wheezing, he reached over and opened the glove compartment. Two keys linked by a metal ring lay on top of the owner's manual. Standish slid them out.

He inserted a key into the ignition, turned it, and stepped on the accelerator. All these actions seemed to be remembered from some other, very different, past life. He heard the engine catch, and dropped his forehead to the wheel and rested. Another great chunk of Esswood fell onto the roof. Standish forced himself to straighten up. He put the car in reverse and stepped on the accelerator. The Escort smashed into the half-opened doors and rolled out. Standish cut the wheel and turned the car forward. Shreds and dots of fire rained down from the house. Standish jammed the car into drive and floored the accelerator. The car mushed up a spray of gravel and shot forward. Red light wavered on the drive and the tall straight oaks. Steam hissed from the trunks of the trees closest to the house. Standish turned on his lights, and streams of yellow floated into the wavering red night. He saw the long drive curling away between the steaming trees, and he aimed for it.

Then he was rolling down the drive, trying to figure out which side he was supposed to be on. Everything was *backward*.

A pair of headlights appeared before him down through the tunnel of trees at the bottom of the drive. Standish let the accelerator drift upward while he tried to solve the interesting problem of which side of the road was his. He swerved all the way left, then right. The oncoming car flicked its lights off and on. In the rearview mirror, Esswood blazed merrily. The other car moved into his headlights. It was a Jaguar, and Robert Wall—"Robert Wall"—was driving it. Standish's beloved, his sister, sat beside him. Both of Edith's children looked startled, perhaps even transfixed. Robert honked his horn and waved at Standish. His beloved spoke words he could not hear. Standish drove on. When he went past the Jaguar, Robert yelled at him and his beloved leaned forward and questioned him with her eyes. Standish picked up speed. Neither one had recognized him.

After a couple of seconds Standish looked in the rearview mirror and saw Robert Seneschal running down the drive after him. He moved his head to see himself in the mirror. He did not recognize himself either. He was a totally new being, bald, covered with grease and blood, pink and blue-eyed: he was his own baby. The car shot out into the road at the end of the drive, and grinning giggling Standish turned the Escort toward the village.

nineteen

After a time the red blur faded from the sky. Standish drove without maps, without memory, guided by a sense of direction that seemed coded into his body. He drove through a landscape of tiny villages filled with cheery lights and flashing signs, of dark fields and dense woods. He saw marsh lights flicker and understood that they too were part of the great sentence that went on forever until it passed from visibility. Every human life fit into that grand and endless sentence. Occasionally he glanced with admiring satisfaction at the newborn baby in the rearview mirror.

He moved swiftly through the villages and fields. Churches, pubs, and thatched cottages went by in the dark. Once he saw a house even greater than Esswood on the crest of a long hill, and Rolls-Royces and Bentleys and Daimlers were drawn up before it, and light spilled from every window. Somnolent cows and horses in the fields swung their heads to watch him pass by.

Once in a deep wood he struck an animal and heard it cry out with a terrible cry.

His hands stiffened and froze to the wheel. Still Standish drove easily through the night. He was a great fat chuckling baby, and he shat and peed in his filthy trousers and kept driving.

At last he came to the open-air factories. The strings of light had been turned off; the torches were put away. The machines rested in the dark passages, and the swirling dust had settled for the night. Yet the great slag heaps rose up into the starry sky, and when Standish saw them he slowed down.

He peeled his right hand from the steering wheel and leaned sideways to crank down the passenger window. When the car drifted alongside the first slag heap, Standish lifted one of the pillowcases and swung it through the window. It struck the road and rolled toward the slag heap. He supposed that was good enough. He tossed the second pillowcase after the first. This one made it nearly across the road before it thumped down and tumbled into a drainage ditch.

Standish groaned and sat up straight again.

Eventually the HUCKSTALL sign flashed in his window and disappeared behind him. Chuckles emanated from the two dripping bags no longer beside him on the passenger seat. An empty world without end or beginning spread out on both sides of the road. Then headlights appeared far ahead down the road. As he drove toward them the figure of a man with outstretched arms stepped forward into the beams of his own lights. Standish was near enough to see in his own headlights that the man was smiling as he waved his arms. The man moved nearer to the center line. He was not what Standish had expected—a tall smiling man in a sport jacket. His fair hair flopped appealingly over his forehead.

Standish accelerated when he drew near to the man, and when the man began crisscrossing his arms over his head—for this one was used to getting what he wanted, you could see it in his wide-set eyes and smooth cheeks—Standish turned the wheel sharply toward the man and ran straight into him.

The man bounced against the car with enough force to jolt Standish painfully against the wheel. He spun off like a marionette and disappeared beneath the car. There came another, milder jolt. Standish braked to a halt and threw open the door. He put the gear lever at park but did not turn off the car. He slid off the seat. With slow determined steps, not bothering to inspect the crushed body beneath the car, the poor baby set off into a wide desolation.